# HALO
# FOR
# SATAN

# HALO
# FOR
# SATAN

Howard Browne

NO EXIT PRESS

1988

No Exit Press
18 Coleswood Road
Harpenden, Herts AL5 1EQ

*British Library Cataloguing in Publishing Data*

Browne, Howard 1980-
    Halo for Satan — (No Exit Press Vintage Crime)
    I.Title
    813'.52[F]

ISBN 0 948353 19 8
ISBN 0 948353 20 1 Pbk

9  8  7  6  5  4  3  2  1

Printed by The Guernsey Press Co. Ltd.,
Guernsey, Channel Islands.

*For*

ALLEN BROWNE

# · 1 ·

He was a big man, big all over, wrapped in a tan Palm Beach suit that appeared to have been cleaned and pressed no more than ten minutes before. He stood with his back against the smoke-blackened front of a florist shop directly across the street from the rectory entrance, just standing there without a thought in his head or a care in the world while he worked on his front teeth with a toothpick, using a strong wrist movement.

The brim of a crisply new Panama shielded his round firmly fleshed face from the midmorning May sunshine, but I caught the dull white shine of eyes watching me from under hooded lids across the distance.

My conscience was clear, so being stared at didn't change my pulse rate. He could have been a cop in plain clothes or a bill collector loafing on company time or only a private citizen with nothing better to do than lean against buildings and make honest folks nervous by giving them the hard eye. I wouldn't have noticed him particularly if the clothing he was wearing hadn't seemed a little out of place for this time of year.

I opened one of a pair of heavy screen doors, went through and into the rectory entrance hall, shadowy and dim, across that and through an arched opening into a large square room paneled in glossy walnut and divided by a counter-top railing in the same wood. On my side of the railing, their backs to the windows, was a row of the kind of chairs you find in waiting rooms everywhere and a bare wooden bench that looked about half as com-

fortable as the chairs. The room smelled a little, I thought,
like the Sunday school hall I hadn't been in since my
twelfth birthday. That had been twenty years ago, though,
and I might be mistaken about it.

I went over and put an elbow on the counter and said,
"Good morning," to an angular woman in her sixties
who was sitting at a typewriter stand at right angles to
a small PBX board.

She was wearing an Oxford-gray suit, very severe in
the lines, and a spotless white blouse featuring a lacy
jabot. There were wrinkles in her face, not too many and
not too deep, and her hair was a good honest shade of
gray drawn tightly back into a roll at the nape of her
neck. With all of this, her eyes were youthful and sharp
and there was strength in the sharp thrust of her chin and
the high-arched lines of a rather prominent nose.

She stood up without creaking and came over to the
railing opposite to where I was standing. Her thin lips,
colorless, moved a little in an impersonal smile. "Good
morning. May I help you?"

"Yes," I said. I brought out my wallet and found one
of my cards, with *Private Investigations* in small neat
script in the lower left-hand corner, and handed it to her.
"Bishop McManus. I have an appointment."

The card seemed to fascinate her. She stood there
staring down at it, her dry lips moving a little as she
silently repeated the printed words. There was faint color
in her cheeks where color hadn't been a moment before
and her breathing was a trifle unsteady. I wondered what
all this was leading up to.

Finally she put the card down on the counter and
pushed it gently toward me with a short-nailed forefinger.
Her faded blue eyes were having trouble focusing on
mine.

"Private investigations." Her voice quavered ever so
lightly. "Does that mean you're a detective, Mr. Pine?"

"Just the private kind," I said. "I couldn't arrest
anybody, if that's what you mean."

Her blue-veined hand jerked a little on the counter and very quickly she dropped it to her side. "I certainly didn't mean any such thing! Why should you think that?"

I gave her a hearty smile. "I hardly know myself. It just seemed something to say."

It failed to reassure her. She brought her hand back up and fidgeted it along the railing, looked past me at the row of chairs, then back to me again. The impersonal smile was completely gone now, possibly forever, leaving a pinched look to her mouth and worry in her eyes.

She began to speak very quickly, the words telescoping. "I've worked for him for twenty-two years this coming August, Mr. Pine, and I feel I have the right——" She brought up her hand suddenly and pressed hard against the flesh under the right side of her chin. "I—I'm not making much sense, am I, Mr. Pine?"

"I don't know," I said. "You'll have to say a little more, one way or the other, before I can tell."

She looked quickly around the room again. Nobody there. There hadn't been before and there wasn't now. Just she and I, cozily together. My soothing smile was becoming forced.

"He's been acting so strangely, Mr. Pine. Ever since he came back from New York. Three days ago. Something is worrying him. Terribly. He seems older and thinner and there are new lines in his face. He won't see anyone, Mr. Pine, or hardly even talk to them on the telephone. Just sits up there in his office and worries. He canceled all his appointments and is completely neglecting his Church duties. The day he came back he called up and told Father Kelly, his secretary, to take his vacation immediately. He's terribly worried, Mr. Pine. And now he's sent for a detective!"

This could go on for hours. I said, "Maybe you'd better let the Bishop know I'm here. It sounds like every minute counts."

The words went over her head and shattered soundlessly against the wall. She went right on, looking at me

without seeing me, getting it all out before it choked her.
"It's none of my business, of course, Mr. Pine. But I've
been in this office more than twenty years and I can't
bear to see him so worried. If only he would . . . What
did you wish to see him about, Mr. Pine?"

I said gently, "It's the other way around. He wants
to see me. I have an appointment." I put the ball of my
thumb on the card and pushed it half an inch toward her.
"Remember?"

She looked vaguely at the thumb, a little surprised at
seeing it there. "Certainly I remember. I'm afraid I'm
just a meddlesome old woman who talks too much."
She blinked at me wanly and worked up a smile that was
bankrupt before it was born. "I've certainly run on,
haven't I? I do hope you won't say anything to him
about . . . He's such a good man, really, and I hate to
see . . ."

"Not a word," I said.

"You're very understanding, Mr. Pine."

"It's the least I can do."

She snuffled once and beamed damply at me. "Thank
you. If you'll be seated for a moment. His wire is busy."

She turned and went back to the switchboard while I
was drifting over to the nearest chair.

Time passed, dragging as it does when you're waiting.
I sat there in the center of a square of strained sunlight
slanting in through a stained-glass window behind me
and dangled my foot over the other knee. I divided my
time between counting squares in a design of the heavy
linoleum and analyzing the features of a red-hatted cardinal staring sternly at me out of black eyes in a life-
size oil painting on the opposite wall.

The PBX buzzed a time or two, but not for me. I
dozed lightly in the sun's pleasant warmth, thinking of
a cigarette but reminding myself that only an unwashed
infidel would smoke in church.

The buzzer sounded again and I got the beckoning

finger. The woman was back to being businesslike; she directed me through a closed door at the far end of the room. "Room 203, Mr. Pine. The stairs are down the corridor, to your left."

Up there the halls were carpeted with some short-piled tough material the color of an old bloodstain, and the doors were veneered in polished walnut, with cream-colored numerals and pearl buttons to push. I found 203 without making a job of it and laid my thumb against the buzzer.

A voice, resonant and deep, the way I imagined a bishop's voice would sound, told me to come in. I pushed open the door and entered with my hat in my hand.

It was a room fitted out as an office by somebody who didn't know how to pinch pennies and who wasn't expected to know how. It was large and square and the ceiling was away up above me. There was soft-piled rose broadloom to the baseboards, white metal Venetian blinds and gold damask draperies at the windows and redwood paneling on the only wall that wasn't lined with shelves of books in rich bindings behind glass. A circular redwood stand in one corner supported a huge globe, and a console radio in the same wood stood across from that. The only visible object to prove this wasn't the office of an oil baron was a large crucifix in the center of that open stretch of wall.

Between the two windows was an oversize redwood desk supporting a lamp in dull bronze, a brown desk blotter trimmed in tan leather and gold, a white-marble pen set and a bronze ashtray big enough to bathe a camel in.

There was a man in the tan leather swivel chair behind the desk. He leaned back and watched me blaze a trail through the carpeting; then he gave me a grave smile and said, "Good morning, Mr. Pine. I'm Bishop McManus. I appreciate your coming. Please sit down."

It appeared he wasn't the type to shake hands with the

hired help. I took the redwood and tan leather chair across the desk from him, placed my hat on a corner of the desk and, taking my cue from the ashtray, got out my cigarettes.

The Bishop sat there and watched me get one burning, his strong square hands locked loosely across his slight paunch. When he saw that I was comfortable and waiting he unclasped his fingers and bent forward to push aside the lamp and get a better view of me.

He said crisply, "Calling you yesterday afternoon, Mr. Pine, was something of an impulse on my part. By that I don't mean I've begun to regret doing so; but I would like to know something about you before I go further into my . . . problem."

I blew smoke through my nose and got down to being cooperative. "I'm thirty-two, reasonably strong and, considering the life I lead, unreasonably healthy. I vote the Democratic ticket—when I vote at all. I was an investigator for the State's Attorney here in Chicago for a couple of years. For the past two years I've been in business for myself in a small way as a private investigator. I can give you as references the names of some people you probably know."

I got another of his grave smiles. "It takes time to check references, Mr. Pine. Somehow or other I had the opinion we'd met before, but you corrected me on that during our telephone conversation yesterday. In my work, however, I've learned to evaluate people quickly and with reasonable accuracy. Instead of checking references I'm going to rely on that, since time is so important in this matter."

He stopped there and rubbed a palm over the hairy back of his other hand, his mild blue eyes fixed on the crucifix behind me. "What I would like you to do for me is undoubtedly simple for someone in your line. I want a man located. But the reason I want him located is completely incredible."

He closed his eyes briefly and gave a short rapid shake to his head as though faintly surprised to find himself discussing the matter at all. I knocked cigarette ash into the bronze tray and crossed my legs the other way. At the rate he was getting his story out, that tray wasn't going to be too big after all.

Even without the reversed collar and black dickey he would have looked the part of a clergyman. He was of medium height, with a build that had started out to be fat and ended up as heavy-set, the kind of build you find so often in men around his age. His bushy black hair was going to be entirely gray before his bald spot caught up with it, and he wore it combed straight back, although from the way it separated along one side I judged he had parted it at that point until recently. It seemed even bishops were sensitive about losing their hair.

His face was round and inclined to puffiness about the eyes and under the chin. There were wrinkles at the corners of his eyes and a few near his mouth. They didn't seem to be new wrinkles either, no matter what the nice old woman downstairs had said. That got me to wondering how you would tell an old wrinkle from a new one.

Bishop McManus put a hand against the desk edge and pushed himself deeper into his chair, sighing a little. "To be truthful, Mr. Pine, I'm not even sure he is missing. Your work may amount to nothing beyond delivering a message to this man at the address he gave me."

"Only," I said, "you think maybe he isn't there any more."

He nodded with slow emphasis. "Exactly. If he ever lived there at all."

"His name and the address he gave you will do to start with," I said. "If he's there I won't have to know why you want him found. If you'd rather have it that way."

He considered it while doing a little finger tapping on

the arm of his chair. "No, Mr. Pine. If I'm going to hire you, I'm going to trust you. I simply can't send you into a situation like this half informed." His eyes came up to my face and there was a glint in them that hadn't been there before. "You see, I have every reason to believe there is an element of danger in the matter—a strong element of danger."

If I hadn't appeared impressed it would have disappointed him. So I put a troubled line in my forehead and said, "I've worked on a job or two that turned out on the rocky side. It's always nice to know in advance."

He blinked somberly at me. "It seemed only fair to warn you. If you feel you'd rather not get involved . . ." He let it hang there, waiting to learn how much of the iron in me was rust.

I gave him a big courageous smile to show that neither rain nor snow nor deep of night could keep Paul Pine from earning his living, such as it was. "Let me give it a whirl. Maybe it won't be as bad as you think."

The Bishop sighed in his small way and made a tent of his forefingers and nudged his lower lip with it while making up his mind. Dust motes danced in the spring sunlight streaming in at the open windows and a soft breeze from the lake, five blocks to the east, stirred the ashes in the tray.

"Ten days ago," the Bishop said abruptly, "a man came here to see me. I was in New York at the time and the receptionist downstairs told him I would not be back for another week. He wanted to know the exact date I would be in my office, then left without giving his name."

He bogged down again and went back to prodding his lower lip, his eyes on the crucifix beyond my left shoulder.

"That's interesting," I said, trying to get him started once more.

Nothing got by him. He glanced sharply at me, the

light shining along his blue eyes. "Not yet it isn't Mr. Pine. Please be kind enough to bear with me if I seem a little slow in telling this. I'm not altogether sure I should be telling it at all."

It was my first look behind the benign facade of Bishop McManus. I began to understand that there was a mind sharp enough to shave with behind those mild blue eyes, that his grave smile went no deeper than his teeth, that the only flabby thing about him was the wrapper he came in.

I looked at the toe of my shoe and thought of my bank balance. It didn't take much thought; it wasn't much of a balance.

Now that I had been put in my place, the Bishop was ready to go on with his story. "He was here, waiting downstairs, the day I returned. He insisted on talking with me in private. I brought him up here.

"His name was Raymond Wirtz, although he is using another name where he is staying. He sat there where you're sitting now, Mr. Pine, and said he had something he wanted to sell me."

I said, "Let's go back a little way if you don't mind. Tell me what Wirtz looks like and your general impression of him."

"About your own height, Mr. Pine, but rather on the frail side. My first impression that he was a professional man of some kind was borne out by what he told me during our conversation. In his late forties, I think, although the state of mind he was in made him appear older. Thin in the face, brown hair, thinning a little at the temples. A fairly handsome man under normal circumstances, I would say."

"That's twice," I said, "you've commented on something other than his physical appearance. Go into that a little deeper, if you will."

He put one hand over the back of the other and squeezed the knuckles while fixing his eyes on the line of smoke from my cigarette. When he spoke, his voice seemed curiously deeper.

"The man was frightened half out of his wits, Mr. Pine. He was nervous, jumpy, constantly on edge all the time he was here."

"All right," I said. "Tell me the rest of it in your own way. I won't interrupt again."

Bishop McManus turned in the swivel chair to stare out the window at nothing at all. "When he told me he had something to sell, I'm afraid I got a bit blunt with him. He cut off my protests sharply by saying, as nearly as I can recall his exact words, 'I'm not selling prayer books or rosaries, Your Grace. This is a single item and the only one of its kind. And the price is such that I would go directly to the Vatican if it were at all possible.' "

"With a build-up like that," I said, "any amount under a million is going to sound mighty puny."

He turned his head to learn the effect his next words would have on me. "Precisely. But a million dollars was not the price, Mr. Pine." He moved one hand in a slow graceful motion. "The amount he asks is twenty-five million dollars!"

If he was trying to stun me he succeeded. I got my lower jaw up off my necktie and said weakly, "That should kick quite a hole in the petty cash."

It earned me another of his grave smiles. "The amount is preposterous, of course. When he mentioned such a figure I knew I was dealing with a madman or a crank. My only thought was to get rid of him as quickly and with as little fuss as possible. Humoring him seemed to be the best way. So I asked him what he had that could possibly be worth such a fantastic price. And he told me."

I was going to get stunned again. I could feel it coming. I waited seven seconds to help build up suspense before I said, "What was he selling?"

"A manuscript, Mr. Pine. Written by Our Lord, Jesus Christ."

It might have been the honest awe in his voice, or maybe I'd been sitting too long in one place. But right then there was a prickly feeling along my spine and a lifting sensation to the hair on the back of my neck.

I sat there staring at the Bishop while traffic sounds floated up from Wabash Avenue below the open windows and an airplane motor hummed from far off. For a moment I had the crazy feeling that I was looking at His Grace across an acre of sun-flooded water.

I blinked a time or two to dispel the illusion, and said, "My religious training has been a little sketchy. But somewhere along the line I picked up the impression that Our Saviour left no written records."

"Exactly, Mr. Pine. To the Church's knowledge, no such manuscript exists."

"Yet Wirtz says differently. Is there even a small chance he's right?"

The Bishop spread his hands. "Almost certainly he is wrong. But you see the position it puts me in."

"If what he's got is what he says, would you pay twenty-five million for it?"

He said solemnly, "Such a document cannot be valued in dollars and cents, Mr. Pine. Its spiritual significance, the veneration in which so holy an object would be held, its possible effects on the canons of Christianity itself . . ." His voice trailed off and his shoulders rose in a shrug to indicate this was something beyond words.

"Did he show you the manuscript?"

"Oh, no. If I expressed a willingness to use my good offices to effect a sale at his price, he would agree to bring it here the following day."

I ground what was left of my cigarette against the side of the bronze ashtray and got out another and moved it around in my fingers without lighting it. I said, "Where did Wirtz get hold of this thing in the first place?"

*John Evans*

"He didn't say, Mr. Pine. And I didn't ask him."

"As far as that goes," I went on, "how does he know it's what he claims it is? Wouldn't a thing like that be pretty difficult to identify?"

He nodded, his eyes fixed on the cigarette dancing in my fingers. "You've hit on the real reason for my not ordering Wirtz out of this office early in our conversation. You see, Mr. Pine, Wirtz is an accredited paleographer."

I blinked at him. "That means what?"

"Wirtz claimed to be one of the four leading experts on ancient papers and inks in the world. He holds—or held, I'm not sure which—a position of some sort with the University of Southern California, and does a great deal of work for museums, universities, private collectors and business firms."

"He just tell you that, or what?"

"He showed me letters and cards. They appeared to be authentic."

"Did he describe this document to you?"

"Briefly. He said it consisted of eight sheets of yellowed parchment, covered with faded but still legible script written in Aramaic."

"Would that be in line?"

"The tongue spoken by Jesus was Aramaic, Mr. Pine."

I put the cigarette in my mouth and lighted it. My fingers were steady; nothing had happened so far to make them shake. "You told me earlier that Wirtz is using an assumed name. What is it?"

"Walsh. Raymond Walsh."

"Did he show you anything else besides those letters and cards you mentioned to prove he was really Wirtz?"

"Yes. At his own suggestion. An old draft card bearing his signature. Also a driver's license."

"An Illinois license?"

"No. California. He's been in Chicago less than two weeks."

"What make was the car? If you noticed."

"I noticed, Mr. Pine," he said dryly. "I made it my business to notice. The license was for a Chevrolet coupe. I don't recall the year."

"You remember the address it showed for his home?"

"Hillrose Avenue, I think. I've forgotten the exact number. I suppose I should have written it down."

I was getting needles in my legs. I got up and walked over to the window and looked down into Wabash Avenue. The big guy in the Palm Beach suit was still holding up one corner of the florist shop but the toothpick was gone. It seemed an improvement. Nothing else around but sunshine and two women in house dresses going into a grocery store. Not that I was interested.

Behind me I heard the swivel chair creak faintly. The Bishop said, "What are you thinking, Mr. Pine?" He sounded more than slightly worried.

I went back to my chair and sat down again. "I hardly know. What arrangement did you and Wirtz decide on, Your Grace?"

"Simply that I would like to examine this document and that if it turned out to be authentic—which I told him was hardly likely—the Church would definitely be interested in buying it."

"And?"

"He agreed to bring it in the following day. Said I was free to make any tests I saw fit, but that once I was satisfied the document was authentic he would expect the Church either to meet his price or return his property."

"That seems fair enough."

His fingers tightened suddenly on the arm rests of his chair. "Mr. Pine, it is incredible that such a manuscript could exist, certainly not a genuine one. Had I thought for a moment it were at all possible, I would not have telephoned you. It's only that . . . well, any possibility, however slight . . . I keep thinking . . ."

His voice flickered out entirely and he sat there watching me rub my chin while I picked over the information he had furnished. I understood why he, for all his grave smile and calm manner, was as jittery underneath as an elephant on stilts. His fear of missing the chance to get his hands on that hunk of papyrus was keeping him tight to his office, not to mention adding years to his age and fresh wrinkles to his face. With a thing like this brewing he wasn't able to go about the bishop business. No wonder he had canceled all appointments and sent his secretary away: it wouldn't do to have other ears hanging open in the vicincity.

I said, "You mentioned a while back that Wirtz was having a bad case of nerves. Any idea what was chewing on him, other than owning something worth so much money?"

"You've probably answered your own question, Mr. Pine. Although Wirtz was more than a bundle of nerves. There was a bitterness in him too—a cynical attitude. It led me to believe someone had done him a terrible injustice at one time or another. Such was my impression."

"Yeah. When he failed to show that second time, what did you do about it?"

"Nothing. Nothing at all. My first reaction was that Wirtz had been a crank after all. But I couldn't get the whole affair out of my mind; it came to the point where I could think of nothing else. Yet I could hardly go out there myself, and certainly I could send no one from the Church." The vertical line between his eyes deepened. "I hope it will be no more complicated than just your going out to see him. Wirtz hinted that men already have died over possession of the manuscript. That is why I mentioned this might prove a dangerous assignment."

I ground out my cigarette and watched the black ashes crawl in the faint breeze from the window. "I don't rate the danger very high," I said. "This sounds like a fancy con game to me and I'll enjoy proving it. If I should run across any manuscript that looks older than yesterday's newspaper, I won't go south with it. Having twenty-five million dollars would scare the pants off me.''

That brought me another of his grave smiles. ''You've expressed my own feelings, Mr. Pine. I have every confidence that you'll handle this matter intelligently.''

''Thank you. If you'll let me have the address I'll take a run out there and do what I can. For a quick guess I'd say Wirtz got a little scared at the score he was trying to run up on this caper and took a powder.''

Bishop McManus looked at me with his mouth open about an inch and bewilderment in his mild blue eyes. I said, ''Just my way of talking, Your Grace. I mean the enormity of what he was trying to do must have frightened him off. Sometimes I sound like a bad movie.''

''I see.'' He still sounded doubtful but let it go at that. He drew open the center drawer of the desk and took out a small white card and a fountain pen with gold filagree work along the sides. While I was admiring the pen he filled in the card with two lines of small cramped script and handed it to me. The name Raymond Walsh was first and under that an address in the seventeen hundred block on West Erie.

I flicked a thumbnail against the underside of the card. ''For a man worth twenty-five million bucks, Wirtz certainly lives in a cheesy neighborhood. You can just about buy a square block around there for the price of a ready-made suit.''

''So I understand.'' He returned the fountain pen to the drawer and closed it again. ''There was a sort of threadbare neatness about the man. I don't imagine even a leading paleographer earns a great deal of money, Mr. Pine. That reminds me.''

He bent with an effort and pulled out the right-hand bottom drawer of the desk and came up with a green metal cashbox which he put carefully down on the blotter pad. ''You'll want to be paid, of course. I'm afraid I neglected to ask your fee.''

''In your case,'' I said, ''that can come later. I get

thirty dollars a day, which includes expenses. It doesn't seem so much any more, after hearing all this talk about millions. I haven't had many cases where the talk got into even the thousands. I can bill you, Your Grace, when the job is finished, or when you decide there's no further point in keeping me on the job.''

He shook his head briefly. ''I prefer to pay in advance, if you don't mind.'' A key from a pocket chain unlocked the box. He folded back the lid, took out a comfortably thick sheaf of bank notes and counted out two fifties, two twenties and a ten, all of them crisp as the day they left the presses.

''This will cover five days of your time,'' he said, handing them to me. ''If you conclude the matter satisfactorily before then, you may regard the difference as a bonus.''

I said something about that being very handsome of him and tucked the bills into my wallet. The four singles already in there looked mortified and tried to crawl under the lining.

The Bishop finished locking the cashbox and returned it to the drawer. He stood up then to indicate the interview was over and came around to open the door for me.

I said, ''I'll let you know as soon as I have something to report.''

''Good.'' He smiled and put out his hand. ''I've enjoyed meeting you, Mr. Pine. You see, you're the first— ah—private eye I've come in contact with.''

''That sort of evens us up,'' I said. ''You're my first Bishop.''

We shook hands and I went off down the corridor, leaving him standing there.

I walked down to the first floor, ignored the pleading glance of the woman at the PBX board, and went on out into the shallow entrance hall with its composition flooring of alternate black and white squares and matching bronze busts of a pope and a cardinal, and out into Wabash Avenue. The big guy was still lounging across the street, reading a paper now or at least looking at the pictures.

June was still two weeks away but spring had come earlier to Chicago this year and the late morning sun was bright and hot. The street parkway strips were as green as they would ever be and the few trees in this part of town were going to have leaves any day now.

I went around the corner to where the Plymouth was parked at the curb on Superior Street. This had been a fashionable neighborhood once, but that was seventy years ago and the two and three-story residences had the faintly decayed look that goes with gas mantels and charcoal bed warmers. Somewhere a robin sang lustily and there was the evenly spaced whacking sound of a rug being beaten over a clothesline.

It would have suited me fine to stand there and breathe in the soft spring air and think how nice it was to be working again, this time for a client who hadn't started out by trying to tear my head off or by asking me to wait for my money until an erring husband got around to making his alimony payments.

But His Grace had a problem which was now my problem as well, and the answer lay in another part of town.

I crawled in behind the wheel of the Plymouth and started out for the seventeen hundred block on West Erie Street.

# ·2·

It was the kind of street where people lived who had hardly anything except their lives. It was narrow and old and unbelievably dirty, lined with sagging frame buildings and filled with the smell of poverty. Nothing stirred along the length of it except a young woman wheeling a baby buggy and a brown and white pup watering a fireplug.

Number 1730 was three floors and an English basement of frayed and weary wood that had been painted gray and trimmed in blue about the time Grant was writing his memoirs. Cracked green shades hung limply behind tightly closed windows, with an occasional curtain of white net to point up the surrounding squalor. Rusty iron railings leaning at an angle flanked a flight of worn wooden steps from the sidewalks to the first floor.

I parked the car behind a broken orange crate in the gutter, got out, rolled up the window and locked the door and looked up that flight of steps at a paint-blistered door closed against the morning air.

An old man was sitting on the top step soaking sunshine into his bones and a gray-fringed bald spot. A yellow corncob pipe smoldered between relaxed fingers resting on one knee, and his blue work shirt was tucked carelessly under the belt line of a shapeless pair of faded blue denims.

We stared into each other's eyes across the distance. Very slowly he lifted the pipe from his knee and put its stem into the opening under the gray blob of his nose. I tipped a hand at him and went up the steps two at a time, just to show off.

He blinked watery blue eyes at the handkerchief in my breast pocket when I stopped a step below him, and then said, "Lookin' for someun, young feller?" around the pipestem.

"In a way," I said. "Kind of hot, hunh?"

He allowed it was hot, all right, but said he liked it that way at his age. That seemed invitation enough, so I sat down next to him on the step and got out my cigarettes and lighted one. I could smell his pipe and I could smell him a little. A dry musty-clean smell like a bar of yellow laundry soap.

I blew smoke through my nose and locked my hands around one knee. After a moment of silence, I said, "You the landlord around here?"

He turned his head and looked placidly at the bridge of my nose where a football cleat had put a dent back in my high-school days. "No, sir," he said stiffly. "I don't own no propitty and I don't aim to, neither. Man don't rightly own propitty I allus say. It owns him."

He could never convince me he spoke from experience on that score but it hardly seemed worth debating. "You live here, though?"

"Sure. I live here. Right nice place for livin' long's you don't own it."

"You know the other tenants?"

"Some I do, some I don't. They come and go."

"There's a man named Walsh. Could we talk about him a little?"

He took the corncob pipe out of his mouth, eyed it as if he had never seen it before, then put it back with thoughtful care and took three slow puffs, the gray smoke climbing straight up in the still air. He said, "Mebbe we could. Depends."

"On what?"

"On where it takes us. You a law man, mister?"

"Not the way you mean," I said. I picked a splinter from the edge of the step and drew lines on the back of my left hand. "This is for his own good."

He thought about that while his eyes went over the collection of bumps and hollows that make up my face.

Finally he grunted deep in his throat and said, "Seems you're tellin' it straight. I seen that Walsh feller a time or two. A mixed-up man, mister. You got a name?"

"Pine," I said. "How's he mixed-up?"

"Worried." The old man nodded judiciously. "Somethin's pushing him hard. I wouldn't know what."

"What did he say to make you think that?"

"Man don't have to talk to tell you he's worried."

I nodded to that. The splinter broke in half and I dropped the pieces over the railing next to me. A delivery boy went by on a bicycle, its wire basket filled with beer bottles.

I said, "He was around to see a man and arranged to go back again. But he never showed, so the man sent me around to find out why."

He took the pipe from between his teeth, this time to spit over the railing. "Ain't seen him around last three, four days. Miz Trotter would have told me had he moved out though."

"She the landlady?"

"Yep. Unhappy woman, mister. Worries about her propitty." He shifted a little on the decaying wood. "Walsh got a room on the third floor, in front, left side. You might go knock on the door."

I stood up and dusted the seat of my pants and stepped on my cigarette. "It's an idea." I took out a dollar and tucked it into the fist holding the pipe. "For your time," I said when he eyed the bill doubtfully.

"Right sure you can spare this, son?"

I put out my hand. "Give it back and the hell with you."

He cackled more than the gag was worth, showing yellow stumps that had been teeth about the time I was in rompers. "First money I ever got just for talkin'. Come around any time, young feller."

I shoved open the front door and went into a gloomy hall filled with last year's air. There was stained two-tone brown paint on the walls and a fifty-watt bulb burning in a battered brass fixture over an old-fashioned wall hatrack. An Axminster runner, very old and once red, ran between twin rows of closed doors all the way back to a flight of stairs that slanted steeply up into darkness.

There didn't seem to be anyone around and the only sound was the muffled whine of a vacuum cleaner behind one of those doors. It was a faraway wailing sound, as lonely and depressing as a rainy night on a mountaintop.

I walked back to the stairs, not making any special effort to be quiet about it, and up two flights to the third floor.

Outside the door that should have been Wirtz's was a cast-iron garbage pail. I lifted the lid and looked in, my only light coming from another fifty-watt bulb a few feet away. There was nothing in the pail but a bad smell. I wondered why I had bothered to look at all. I put the cover back and rapped against one of the door's tobacco-colored panels.

Nothing happened. I tried again, louder this time, but all it earned me was echoes and sore knuckles. I leaned against the door and rattled the knob by turning it all the way . . . and walked in.

It wasn't much of a room. About large enough to play solitaire in if you held the cards close to your chest. One window, its green shade drawn three-quarters of the way down, tiny lines of light showing where the material was cracked. Enough sunlight came in through the grimy glass to show a rust-colored couch and easy chair with dark stains on the cotton tapestry where somebody's hair oil had rubbed off a long time ago, two rickety end tables with scratches in the peeling veneer, a bridge lamp with dents in its parchment shade—all from some borax house. The blue Wilton rug had less nap to it than a cue ball. There was a curtained alcove between a closet door, closed, and an inadoor bed turned into the wall.

It seemed I would have to come back another day to see Mr. Wirtz. Still, as long as I was here, there would be no harm in my looking around. If nothing else I might come across the manuscript. Not that I could do much more than touch it a little. Still it would be fun to touch twenty-five million dollars. A man could spend the rest of his days bragging about a thing like that.

The more likely places gave up nothing but a cheap brier pipe, a half-filled chamois tobacco pouch, two matchbook covers advertising a brand of chewing gum, an electric razor with a crack in the white plastic casing, two halves of a broken black shoelace and a quarter acre of dust. Those last two items were under the couch and I left them there.

No manuscript. Not even a letter from home. I stood up and beat dust from my knees and looked around for new worlds to conquer. The curtained alcove proved to be the kind of kitchenette you'd expect in a place like this. That left the closet and the recess holding the inadoor bed. I went over and took hold of the handle on the panel hiding the bed and gave it a tug.

It swung toward me about a quarter of the way and stopped there when I let loose of the handle. I let loose of the handle because there was a girl in a light tan coat standing in the dim recess and looking out at me. Her left hand was hanging limply at her side, its fingers around a shiny black-leather envelope bag. Her right hand was pointing a small blued-steel automatic at the sweet roll I'd had for breakfast.

"Hello there," I said brightly. It took a little while to get the words out because they had to come all the way up from the cuffs of my trousers.

She said, "Get out of my way." Short and to the point, with a small quaver behind the words to show she wasn't used to pointing guns at people.

I backed away slowly, stopping when I came up against one side of the easy chair. The girl came out of the recess then, watching me out of eyes as cold and distant as stars in a winter sky. She circled me warily, keeping the gun aimed at my middle. I turned to keep her in view. She didn't tell me not to. The hall door was where she was going and the gun was to keep me from going along.

She had her hand on the knob when I said, "Haven't you forgotten something?"

It stopped her like running into a wall. She stared hard at me, indecision and suspicion fighting it out on the lovely battleground of her face. She would have loved for me to go on and say what it was she had forgotten. I wasn't going to, though—not until she asked me.

Somewhere a toilet flushed and water whispered in hidden but not soundproofed pipes. I ran a finger gently along the back of the easy chair and watched the girl make up her mind.

She said, "I haven't forgotten anything and you know it. You just want to keep me here."

"Pshaw," I said. "Why would I want to do a thing like that?"

A corner of her lip got chewed while she thought that one over. She seemed to have forgotten the gun in her hand, but not enough to stop pointing it at me.

"All right," I said, "I'll tell you what you've overlooked. It's three floors, not counting the English basement, to the street. The minute you get out of here all I have to do is raise that window and start yelling. That will bring out a lot of people and they'll grab you sure. Then the boys in blue will come and arrest you for going around pointing a gun at folks."

"You wouldn't dare do a thing like that," she snapped.

"You'd have to tell the police what you were doing sneaking around in another man's apartment."

"I'll bet I can think up a better reason than you can. Shall we try?"

She stiffened a little at my tone. "I was waiting for Mr. Walsh. *If* it's any of your affair."

"Behind the bed?" I sneered politely. "Why not under the couch?"

"It's certainly none of your business where I wait for him." She moved away from the door and peered at me. "Just who are you anyway?"

I peered back at her. It was a pleasure to do so. She wasn't twenty-five, although this was the year it could happen. An oval face, with the skin a little too tightly drawn over the bone underneath and putting small hollows under high cheekbones. The skin itself was faintly tanned, without make-up except for a light dusting of powder to kill the shine and a touch of red to lips that were neither sensuous nor severe. Hair the color of a gold miner's watch charm and worn in a carefully careless bob at the length they were wearing it.

The rest of her went well with the face. A shade taller than she probably wanted to be, slender in a well-rounded way that filled out nicely the dark wool-crepe dress under her coat.

The gun came up two inches and her blue eyes, so dark they were more nearly violet, narrowed almost imperceptibly. "Who are you?" she said again, an edge to her voice now.

I said, "I'm just a man named Pine. Nobody to worry about. Hardly worth a first thought, let alone a second. Why don't you put away that gun?"

She smiled. Suddenly. For no reason at all that I could see. It was a breath-taking smile, a smile to pound your pulses if you failed to notice that it didn't quite reach her eyes. I leaned against the chair as some of the tension went out of my legs.

She said, "As a matter of fact, I heard you outside the door. You were just furtive enough to make me— well—hide. In a place like this you never know."

She put the gun in her bag with a casual movement and smiled at me again. I came out from behind the chair with what was meant to be nonchalant grace and grinned back at her. We were now a couple of nice people who had happened to bump into each other under peculiar circumstances.

I said, "I'm waiting for Mr. Walsh myself. Why don't we sit down and wait for him together?"

She pushed back the sleeve of her coat and was a little too showy about consulting a tiny wrist watch in white gold. "I'm afraid not," she said, frowning charmingly at the hour. "I've wasted too much of the morning as it is." She looked up and gave me a flashing, comradely smile. "If you're staying, would you mind telling him Eve Bennett stopped by about the money? He'll understand."

"I'll bet he will," I said.

Her breath snagged slightly and the bright smile slid away. After an awkward pause she said, "Yes. Well, good-by and thank you, Mr. Pine."

She turned her back on me and had taken one step toward the door when I reached out and yanked the leather bag out of her hand.

It brought her around and at me like a slapped panther. "Give me that, damn you!"

My shoulder got in the path of her hand. I said, "Hunh-uh," and backed out of reach while I opened the bag and dug into its contents.

I removed the magazine from the Colt .25, emptied its five cartridges into my pocket and took the sixth one from the chamber. I sniffed at the muzzle without detecting any odor of freshly burned powder, then put back the clip and laid the gun on the chair arm.

The only thing in the bag with a name on it was a bill

from the Stevens Hotel made out to Miss Lola North and covering rental of Room 2212 for the previous week. There was a square compact in gold with a design in brilliants forming the initials LN. Bank notes in a silver clip, a gold-mounted lipstick, a comb, two white handkerchiefs with L worked into the corner of each, a plain black enameled cigarette case and matching lighter, and a few loose bobby pins to match her hair.

She said, "Are you quite finished?" in a voice as tight as a pullman window.

"Uh-hunh." I took up the gun, wiped it off with my handkerchief and let it slide back into the bag. I snapped the catch and bounced the bag lightly on my palm and gave her the cold eye. "I thought you said your name was Eve Bennett?"

Anger was making her look a trifle older but no less lovely. "Either I get that bag or I'll make trouble for you."

"You're in no position to make trouble for anybody." I pointed a thumb at the easy chair. "You look like an intelligent girl, Miss North. Sit down and rest your indignation while we get our facts straightened out."

"I've nothing to say to you."

"Sure you have. Let me tell you why you have. I'm a detective, Miss North. I find you hiding in a room you have no business being in, as far as I can tell. You point a gun at me and try to walk out. Put them together and it fixes things where I have to ask you some questions. I can ask them here or we can go down to the Bureau and talk it over, with a man taking it down in shorthand. Which will it be?"

She gave me a long level stare while indecision flickered in dark eyes deep enough to wade in. "How do I know you're a detective?"

I had been afraid of that. But I dug into a coat pocket and brought out the 1928 deputy sheriff's star I carried to show people who wanted to see a buzzer. I let her have a glimpse of it, being careful to hold the ball of my thumb over the lettering.

She swallowed. "Very well. I have nothing to hide. I thought you were a prowler or something. May I have my bag, please?"

"Sure."

She took it from me and moved up to the lounge chair and sat down, being careful about arranging her skirt.

I crossed over to the couch and rested a hip against one of its arms. Into the silence I said, "Tell me about it, Miss North."

"About what?"

A touch of my tough-guy manner was indicated. "Don't play it cute. I don't have all day."

She threw the point of her chin at me. "I don't see any necessity for your being rude, Mr. Pine."

"I'm being businesslike, not rude. Tell me about it. Were you hiding in there to blast Mr. Walsh when he came in?"

"Certainly not! Of all the idiotic——"

"All right. Don't waste it on me; the movies give me all the acting I can use. What's your business with Walsh?"

She hesitated, then her lips retreated into a straight and stubborn line. "No! You can go right ahead and arrest me. I'm not going to tell you a thing. I'll get a lawyer! I'm not af——"

I said, "That will be all, Miss North. If you're in a hurry, don't let me detain you."

Her eyes opened wide and her mouth went along for the ride. She was surprised—astounded would be a better word—and no acting this time. "You mean I can leave?"

"Uh-hunh. Any time."

"Well . . ." It worried her: I was up to something. "Thank you, Mr. Pine." She got slowly off the chair and stood there, fumbling with the catch of her bag. "I really know hardly anything about Mr. Walsh. A—a friend asked me to stop by. . . ."

"Of course."

She started to say something more, then her lips came tightly together and she walked, with quick nervous strides, to the door and out.

I listened to the sound of high heels click into silence on the uncarpeted stairs. When there was nothing left but quiet, I lighted a cigarette and thought about Lola North. A slip of a girl who could put a flat-footed cop in his place and who was probably proud of doing so. Maybe not, though. Maybe she was worrying a little over how easy the victory had been. And then again, maybe my sheriff's star had been about as impressive as a grapefruit.

A lovely girl, Lola North. Enough figure and not too many years and a face that could come back and haunt you and maybe stir your baser emotions. A girl who could turn out to be pure as an Easter lily or steeped in sin and fail to surprise you either way.

A girl who had been snooping around where twenty-five million dollars was supposed to be.

I dropped my cigarette on the rug and stepped on it, picked up the butt and put it in my pocket, then went over to the wall-bed recess where Lola North had been hiding. There was a line of empty hooks along the back wall and a faint breath of perfume in the air.

I came out into the room again and swung the panel back into place. The closet was all that was left. There would be nothing in there. Go out and have your lunch, Pine.

I went over and opened the closet door.

There was more space in there than I had expected, most of it occupied. Two beat-up traveling bags in black leather stacked in one corner. Shirts, underwear and socks piled neatly on the single shelf. Several four-in-hand neckties in conservative patterns looped around a hanger. Four suits of clothing. But only one of the suits had a body in it.

I leaned against the door jamb, breathing gently and thinking about a girl with warm gold hair and hollows under her cheeks and narrow eyes that were dark-blue and deep enough to wade in. A girl who had told me to go take a flying jump at a Ford, practically, before tilting her nose at my taste in hats and walking out the door. I thought about unnatural death and tough-talking homicide cops and twenty-five million dollars. I began to hate thinking.

The body was suspended by a maroon necktie drawn up under one ear and its ends knotted around one of a row of hooks screwed into a strip of wood against the rear wall. A man's body, hanging there with its back to me, feet against the floor, knees bent, head tilted to one side.

I put a hand gingerly on one of the shoulders and gave it a small tug. The body revolved slowly, showing the front of the neatly buttoned, double-breasted coat to be caked with dried blood, blood that exposure had turned almost black. At the upper edge of the stain was a thin slit in the cloth of the breast pocket. I judged a knife had put that slit in there . . . and the meat beyond it.

The face was other faces I had come across in my day. Strong in the jaw and weak around the mouth. Cunning and stupid and more than a little vicious. The face of a hoodlum.

This had been an old hood, though. The gray in his hair and the lines in his skin put him past sixty. Another item was the heavy coat of tan on the face and hands. It was too early in the season for that kind of tan, which might have meant a winter in Florida or Southern California.

The color of the bloodstains told me enough, but I took hold of one of the dead hands, just to be sure. The skin was cold and damp, and when I moved the arm it swung limp as a spaghetti dinner. I bent and tugged up one of the trouser legs. The skin underneath was purple and the ankle was swollen. Post-mortem lividity in an acute stage. Rigor mortis had come and gone long before, several days before, probably. If Lola North had put a knife in this man it wasn't during today's visit. I didn't think much of the idea anyway. She could hardly have hung the corpse up by the necktie to begin with, then swallowed the knife. Still it was nice to be sure.

I had seen enough . . . enough to indicate that, although the body was in Mr. Wirtz's room, it was not Mr. Wirtz. Not, that is, if the Bishop's description of him had been accurate.

There was any one of several things I could have done. But only one of them made sense. I closed the closet door gently, went out into the hall and down two flights to the first floor.

The old man was sitting within two inches of where I had left him. I stepped out onto the porch and shut the door, banging it more than was necessary, and dropped down next to him. The sun seemed hotter on my back than before and a soft breeze stirred the tangle of old newspapers along the gutters.

I could feel the old man's mild blue eyes watching me while I got out my cigarettes and a folder of matches. He said, "You took a while, son. You make out all right?"

I finished lighting a cigarette, shook out the match, stared at it moodily, then threw it away. "Walsh wasn't at home."

"Uh-hunh." He sucked at his pipe, bringing out a wet bubbling sound but no smoke. I handed over my matches. "Away somewheres, I expect. Else I'd of most likely seen him."

"Tell me something, Pop."

"Try to."

"You see a girl come out of here a couple minutes ago?"

"Yep. Good looker. Real gold hair and a right nice shape on her."

"Did you see her come in ahead of me?"

"Yep."

"How long before?"

"Oh—ten, fifteen minutes likely. No more'n that."

"Ever see her around here before?"

"Can't say's I have."

"Any idea what she wanted?"

"Asked where she could find Walsh. I told her and she went on up."

"Well, for Chrisakes," I growled. "Why didn't you mention her when I asked about Walsh?"

He blinked placidly at me. "None of my business, mister. I can answer a question when it's put to me polite, but that don't mean I feel called on to get gossipy."

"Okay," I said. "If it won't bother your conscience too much, maybe you can tell me about a man. He's around a hundred and fifty pounds, in his sixties, graying brown hair, brown eyes and a tough-tommy front. He might have a room here or he might be a stranger."

He looked off into the distance and thought about it while lighting his pipe. "Sounds about right. Two, three days ago a man like that come around here wantin' to rent hisself a room. Dressed too good for this part o' town, so I kind of suspicioned him."

"He give his name?"

"Not to me. He did most of his talkin' to Miz Trotter."

"But he didn't get a room?"

"Not here he didn't. We're filled up. Miz Trotter told him to try the Meegan's, down at 1707, and he left. Last I seen him."

I clenched my left hand and stared hard at the knuckles. "Well, he's finally found a place: the closet in Walsh's room. Strung up by a necktie and dead as yesterday's ten thousand years."

He jerked his head around sharply and stared at me, blank-faced. "You don't say! How?"

"How what?"

"How'd he get dead? Hung hisself?"

"No. Somebody left him leaning. With a knife. Into the heart. Like dirty fingernails into an overripe watermelon."

The hand holding the pipe twitched a little but nothing showed in his voice. "Kind of upset, ain't you? What do you figger on doin' about it, mister?"

I stood up and looked down at him, hard. "You do only one thing at a time like this, pop. You just call the buttons."

If that made any difference to him, I couldn't see it. I hadn't really thought that it would. He said, "Might use Miz Trotter's phone. First door on your left, inside."

I threw away my cigarette and went back into the shadowy hall and pounded a hand on the proper door. It opened immediately and a withered old woman with yellow skin and lumpy features peered out at me. There was a faded housecoat wrapped primly about her shapeless body and a lacy pink dustcap sat drunkenly on graying hair that probably had already been combed once that month. She looked at me without pleasure and said, "You want something, young man?"

It seemed everybody was throwing my youth at me this morning. I said, "Not that I want to bother you, Mrs. Trotter, but I'll have to use your phone. There's been some trouble."

Suspicion flared in her tight little eyes, suspicion and open hostility. "I don't know about no trouble. This here's a respectable rooming——"

"This can't wait, Mrs. Trotter," I said patiently. "After I make my call I'll be glad to tell you about it."

She dabbed the back of her hand at a stray strand of stringy hair escaping from the dustcap. "You don't set foot in this house until I know what's going on! You think for a minute I let every——"

"It's your house," I said wearily. "There's a dead man in Mr. Walsh's room and the police will want to know about it. Where's your phone?"

That unhinged her lower jaw until I could see a pair of badly fitting store teeth. "Who's dead? Mr. Walsh? How do you know he's dead?"

"A man," I said. "I don't think it's Walsh. The blood ran out of him and hardly anyone can live without blood."

That got the glare it deserved. "You drunk, young man?"

"Pardon me," I said, and put out a foot. She backed away while she was making up her mind not to and I brushed past her and went into a small living room overcrowded with heavy, dark-wood furniture that had been old before Pearl White was making cliff hangers. There was no sign of a telephone and I had to mention it again before Mrs. Trotter pointed to a stand holding a large French doll in a fluffy orange hoop skirt that needed laundering.

I lifted the skirt without blushing, found a cradle-type phone and dialed Central Station. After the operator put me through to Homicide I reported my discovery to a Sergeant DeMuth. He sounded reasonably interested until I mentioned the address, then he asked my name and told me to stick around, that somebody would be along shortly. From his tone I got the impression "shortly" would be about a week.

I replaced the receiver and gave the instrument back to the doll. Mrs. Trotter started to leak questions from every pore but I put her off. Then she wanted to go up and look at the corpse but I discouraged that by saying the cops wouldn't like anybody tramping on the clues. That seemed to run us out of conversation, so I put on my hat and went out the front door.

Pop was still out there, gnawing on the bit of his pipe and looking thoughtfully off into a private world I had no place in. I sat down and stretched my legs. "I guess Mrs. Trotter is a little upset."

He made a vague sound deep in his throat. "I wouldn't wonder. That's what comes of ownin' propitty. Some roomers ain't goin' to take kindly to bein' asked questions by policemen.''

"Any of her roomers handy with a toothpick?"

He squinted at me. "Toothpick, you said?"

"A knife."

"Oh. Never heard it called that. I couldn't rightly say."

I said, "You could do me a favor, pop."

"Like what?"

"Don't mention that blonde to the boys. I'd like to handle that angle myself."

He cackled unexpectedly. "More curves 'n angles to that one, young feller! Mebbe I'd be gettin' myself into trouble, though."

"Forget I asked," I said coldly.

"Don't do no good to get huffy at me, son. If they don't mention her, I won't neither. Best I can do."

"Sorry." I reached for a cigarette, looked at it, sighed and put it back. "That should be enough. I don't think anybody else around here saw her."

He grunted. After a moment he said, "Strikes me kind of funny, Walsh bein' away and a dead man in his room."

"I thought of that," I said.

# · 3 ·

It wasn't more than ten minutes before a gray Mercury Tudor from the West Chicago Avenue station came bulling along Erie with its siren wide open. People, mostly women, began popping out of houses along the street and a crowd had collected even before the squad screeched to a stop across from us.

Two uniform men piled out, crossed over and came quickly up the steps. The one in the lead was no more than twenty-five, if that, with curly black hair showing from under his uniform cap and an olive-skinned face as handsome as a screen star's. He stopped a step or two below the old man and me, gave us an up-and-down stare and snapped out in a tough voice: "Homicide reported at this address. What about it?"

"Third floor, front," I said.

That earned me the chill eye. "Your name Pine?"

"Yeah."

"The report is you found the body. What else do you know?"

"Nothing to speak of," I said.

His expression said I wasn't showing the proper attitude and something would have to be done about it. He was accustomed to having citizens choke up when he did the talking.

"Don't give me that," he said nastily. "Let's have the story and let's have it quick."

I lifted an eyebrow at him. "Aren't you a little out of

your line, Jack? The Bureau boys usually ask the questions.''

He reared back like I'd pulled a gun on him, and
angry color poured into his face. In a suddenly soft
voice he said, ''Well, well. I think we're going to
have fun, buddy. Let's see something with your name
on it.''

''Why, sure,'' I said agreeably. I took out my wallet,
started to hand it to him, then drew back my hand and
emptied the currency compartment of its bills. I gave
him the wallet, and if his face had been red before it was
nothing to what it was now.

He flicked angrily through the identification panels,
then slapped the folder back into my palm. ''Private
snoop, hunh?'' he snarled. ''Too big for your britches
like the rest of your breed. I'll see what I can do for you
in my report.''

The other cop, who had been standing by while all
this was going on, joggled the pretty boy's elbow. He
was an older man, gray at the temples and with the
patiently tough expression that comes with too many
years in the business. He said, ''We better get up there,
Clint, before somebody shows up from Central.''

I finished putting my money back where it belonged,
then took them upstairs and pointed out the body. They
didn't touch anything, just looked around and sneered at
the dust. The gray-haired cop remained behind while his
partner and I went back to the first floor. There was a
zone car parked behind the one from the district, and a
couple of the boys were talking to Mrs. Trotter in the
hall.

On the porch again, I leaned against one of the railings
and watched the crowd in the street. Pop had disappeared
somewhere while I was upstairs and all the company I
had was a plain-clothes man from the zone car. Ten more
minutes dragged by, then a Homicide detail arrived from
Central Station.

The man in charge was a sergeant named Frank Tinney, whom I remembered from the days when he was on a robbery detail. He nodded blankly to me, said, "I won't be long, Pine," and went on through the paint-blistered door. A hell of a lot I cared how long he would be. I had all day. I had three or four days if he wanted them. When the police crook their fingers your private business ceases to be pressing.

I yawned and smoked my cigarette and looked at the empty faces of the crowd.

In less than half an hour, but not much less, Tinney came out again, alone. He said, "Let's you and me talk, hey? How about your car?"

"Okay."

Most of the sight-seers had drifted away by this time and the district and zone cars were gone, leaving a swirl of gas fumes in the air and skid marks on the pavement. I led Tinney over to the Plymouth and we got comfortable in the front seat.

He refused my offer of a cigarette, found two sticks of gum in one of his pockets and began to strip away the wrappers with slow movements of his stubby fingers. He was a tall, raw-boned man in his early forties, with thinning red hair, and an angular homely face full of wisdom and blackheads. After he finished tucking the gum between his molars, he moved his jaw around a time or two and looked at my necktie with faint approval. He said, "How've you been, Pine?"

"Can't complain."

"Keeping you busy?"

"A job here, a job there. Nothing to make me rich."

His gaze wandered from me to the steering wheel, from there to the windshield and on along the dreary vista of Erie Street limp and yielding in the midday sun. He said, "Hell of a neighborhood to die in."

"You know one that isn't?"

"Yeah. You're right, at that." He turned those disillusioned gray eyes back to me. "How about it, Pine? Did you make that guy in the closet?"

"Complete stranger to me," I said. "I'd put him down as a tired muscle."

He nodded. "You're right in there, Pine. Ever hear of Willie Post?"

"Certainly. Louie Antuni's lieutenant. You're not going to tell me that was Willie?"

"So I'm told. Kennedy, one of the boys who came out here with me, pulled him in a time or two back in the old days. He didn't hesitate a minute in identifying him."

I said, "Willie was before my time, back in the days when Taylor Street smelled of sour mash from Jefferson to Robey and was so thick around Halsted Street the school kids could get a cheap jag from inhaling the air. I was sixteen and playing left tackle for Senn High when Louie took that income tax rap." I flicked cigarette ashes out my window. "I'd always heard that Willie stuck with the big boy and was living with him in Florida."

"So everybody says. He couldn't of been in town long, else the Department would of heard about it."

"He still had his Florida tan," I said.

"Yeah. I noticed that."

We sat there and he chewed and I smoked while a minute or two drifted aimlessly by. Finally he stirred on the seat and looked at me with a combination of wariness and solemnity in his eyes. An honest cop, who had come to the place where he must push his weight around some and who was aware that a sergeant's weight is figured in milligrams.

"How do you figure in this, Pine?"

"I hardly figure at all," I said. "I came around to see this man Walsh. I knocked on his door and when he didn't answer I got a little worried and kind of walked in. In looking over the place some I found the body. Naturally I ran for a phone and let you boys know about it."

Tinney's snort was half anger, half envy. "Brother! The things you private guys get away with! Any old time we pull a thing like that our hides would be drying on the wall."

There wasn't any room in that for a remark from me.

He tapped his fingers on his knee and blew out his breath. I could smell the flavor of his gum. "Tell me about this man Walsh."

"I don't know him," I said.

His eyes seemed to grow a bit grayer, a bit bleaker. "You were calling on him, Pine."

"Who says I wasn't? I get paid to call on people I don't know personally."

He bulged out a cheek with his tongue. "I see. A case, hey?"

"Yeah," I said. "A case. A job. I have a client. Knock on wood."

"What's his connection with Walsh?"

"I couldn't say."

Nothing changed in his face. "You know better than this, Pine. I'm not telling you how to run your business and you've got some rights, of course. But this is murder. It's a murder that's going to get a lot of attention around town and I'd like to do a good job of work on it. I could use a boost in rank, and this is my chance."

"I still can't help you," I said. "Much as I'd like to, you understand."

Anger brought a sharp flush to his cheeks and his eyes began to glitter. "Listen to me, goddam it. I got to find Walsh. I talked to that crummy landlady and her cheap-john roomers and all it got me was disgusted. Maybe *you* don't know anything about Walsh, but you'll never in Christ's world make me believe your client don't. He's my only lead and I'm asking you for his name . . . and don't give me none of that crap about 'privileged communications.' I can lock you up if I have to."

"On what charge?" I said, being calm about it.

He shoved out his jaw at me. "Material witness, ob-

structing justice—what the hell do I care? You think I
can't hold you, fella? Listen, I can waltz you around
every outlying station in town until you grow whiskers
down to your socks. How do you like that?''

"I don't like it," I said. "And you won't do it. I'll
tell you why you won't do it. Because it wouldn't get
you a thing. in the first place . . . and because I could
make a trick like that snap back on you.''

He chewed it over, along with his gum. "Okay. You
know all the answers. That's fine.'' His tone and his
scowl said it wasn't fine at all. "And the next time you
want a favor from the Department, you can whistle up
a post. Good-by and bad luck to you!''

He slammed a palm angrily against the door handle
and stepped out onto the curb. Before he could swing
the door shut again, I said, "We could make a deal,
Sergeant.''

It put surprise on his face and froze it there. First I
called his tough talk down to a whisper; now I was talking
deals. I could almost hear the wheels spinning behind
his wrinkled forehead.

"What kind of a deal?'' he said cautiously.

"I'll be looking for Walsh myself and I may find him
ahead of you. If I do you'll get him from me. But if you
beat me to it, I want to know about it immediately and
I want a private talk with him.''

His scowl deepened. "Go to hell. Any old time we
can't get by without your kind of help, I want pictures.''
His arm tensed to slam the door.

"Plus the name of my client," I said.

His hand slid slowly from the edge of the car door
and some of the lines went out of his face, leaving it a
bland mask. "That's more like it.''

"We do business?''

"All you want is a talk with Walsh when we nab
him?''

"Yeah.''

He ran a broad forefinger slowly along the angle of his jaw. "Well, far's I'm concerned, okay. Course, I can't guarantee what the lieutenant'll have to say about it."

"Then go get a note from him," I said coldly. "When you bring it around, we'll make our deal."

He nodded to himself and stared at my right knee while making up his mind. "Okay, Pine, we'll work it out your way."

"One favor," I said. I was enjoying this, although Tinney didn't know it. "Talk to him but don't push him around. I don't want him sore at me."

He moved his shoulders impatiently. "I don't have all day, shamus."

"Uh-hunh." This was going to be one of the high spots in my career. "I'm working on this thing for His Grace, Bishop McManus, Sergeant."

If I had suddenly grown a second head he couldn't have looked at me any differently. At the end of fifteen or twenty seconds he said woodenly, "I find that a little hard to believe, friend. You better let me have some more to go with it."

"No, sir. A deal is a deal. Anything more will have to come from His Grace."

It was a tough one for him to take and his thoughts were spread out on his unhappy face for the world to see. You don't pull in a bishop and stick a light in his eyes and snarl at him. Especially when your name is a good solid Irish name like Tinney. And if you throw it into the lap of your immediate superior and it backfires on *him*, then you're lucky not to be busted down to a patrolman and put to work rattling store doors out in the Kensington district at three in the morning.

He fumbled around, started twice to say something only to have it die in his throat. ". . . I'll see you around, Pine."

"Sure you will. We made a deal."

"Yeah." He eyed me sourly. "Boy, am I lucky!"

Sergeant Frank Tinney closed the car door gently—the best indication yet of his frame of mind—and stepped back onto the sidewalk. I gave him a grave salute, started the motor and pulled away, leaving him standing there.

# · 4 ·

Chicago's Loop is a few acres of skyscrapers encircled by elevated train tracks like an iron wedding ring on the upthrust hand of a giant. A place of big business and little people, of smoke and noise and confusion beyond Babel, where there is satisfaction for every appetite and a cure for every disease.

The Indians lost it a long time ago. The Indians were never luckier.

It was well past noon by the time I came down Wabash Avenue, dodging the el pillars south to Adams Street, and turned in at my usual parking station. A colored attendant in white coveralls slouched over and took the Plymouth away from me. I picked an early edition of the *Daily News* off the corner newsstand, read it over a leisurely lunch at the Ontra, then plodded slowly back through the heat to Jackson Boulevard where I supported a two-room office suite in the Clawson Building, a few doors west of Michigan Avenue.

The Clawson Building was, and is, twelve floors of dirty timeworn red brick dating back to the Columbian Exposition. It was sandwiched between two modern skyscrapers that seemed forever to be trying to edge away from their neighbor. It had a deep lobby, narrow and dim, paneled in gray and white imitation marble, a pair of secondhand bird cages masquerading as elevators and a sullen air of decay. The upper halls smelled like a Kansas hayloft after two weeks of rain, and my fellow tenants ran the type of businesses that attracted more process servers than customers.

The building superintendent, a bitter-faced man who had seen better days and would tell you so, was relieving the regular operator during the lunch hour. He took me up to the eighth floor, wrenching at the controls as though he'd like to pull off the lever and hit me with it, and I walked slowly along the deserted corridor to 812, with my name and PRIVATE INVESTIGATIONS in black on the ground-glass panel.

Inside, the worn brown-leather couch and two chairs were as empty as ever, and nobody had disturbed the stack of magazines on the reed table. I unlocked the inner office door, entered, tossed my hat on one of the two empty brown filing cases against the far wall, picked the morning mail off the tan linoleum under the letter drop and went over to draw up the Venetian blind and open the window a few inches from the bottom.

I lighted a cigarette and set it in one of the ashtray grooves to act as incense against the wet-plaster smell of the room, then got into the cheerfully creaking swivel chair to open my mail. It came to two ads and a perfumed note from a former client whose husband had left her again. The letter suggested I was duty-bound to find the guy, without charge, as it was less than two months since I had dug him out of hiding. It put me in the same category with her watch-repair man.

The ads went into the wastebasket and the letter into the desk's middle drawer. I was going to have to straighten out the contents of that drawer one of these days. Ash Wednesday would be a good day for it. I leaned back and put creases in my chin with a thumb and forefinger and listened to the murmur of traffic from eight floors below and watched the wavering line of cigarette smoke reach for the ceiling. I added up the day's events. I got about as much out of it as I had put in: hardly anything at all.

Not that the morning had been uneventful. A manuscript worth, to one customer at least, twenty-five million dollars; a girl lovely enough to make you gnaw your nails, who was the owner of a gun and a cloudy motive; a gangster from Prohib days who everybody thought was sunning himself in Florida but whose punctured body had turned up hanging by a necktie in an Erie Street flophouse—enough there for a full caldron of trouble. So far, my part in the picture was confined to the role of bewildered spectator. I figured it was time for me to stop wading and begin to swim.

I got out my book of phone numbers from a drawer of the desk, turned to an entry I had made the day before and dialed the number shown. The elderly receptionist put me through to Bishop McManus without question.

He said, "I hardly hoped to hear from you so soon, Mr. Pine. Have you made any progress?"

"Very little. And I'm afraid it won't make for pleasant listening."

After a bottomless pause he said, "Oh?"

"Wirtz," I said, "wasn't at home. He hasn't been, it seems, for the past three or four days. His door was open, though, and I took the liberty of looking around. There was a dead man in his closet."

"Merciful heavens!" He sounded more anxious than startled. "Not Wirtz himself?"

"Not according to the way you described him. Besides, the body has been identified as that of a man named Willie Post."

"Just that? I mean, Mr. Pine, was there anything at all to indicate a connection with Wirtz?"

"Not a smidgen," I said. "Post, as you may recall, had his name in the papers a lot back sixteen years ago. He was Louie Antuni's chief chopper back in the bad old days. The cops seemed pretty wide-eyed about finding him in town. At least the one I talked to was."

"Antuni," the Bishop said thoughtfully. "Chicago's

most notorious gangster. . . . This seems to be getting
quite involved, Mr. Pine. Isn't it generally believed that
Antuni is no longer active? That he is a very sick man
and is in seclusion in Florida?''

"There doesn't seem to be much doubt about that.''
I leaned back and put my heels on the blotter pad and
smiled a little to myself at the thought that maybe His
Grace sat that way now and then. ''No one seems able
to think of any reason for Willie's being back in the big
town.''

The wire hummed faintly for a long moment before
the Bishop spoke again, his voice sounding graver than
before. "What have you done about all this, Mr. Pine?''

"I called the police. You understand, Your Grace, it
was something I had to do.''

"Certainly.''

"Sergeant Tinney of the Homicide detail insisted on
knowing what was behind my call on Wirtz. I refused
to say more than was necessary, but I did give him your
name. I made him work for it, though, and got a small
concession in return which may help. As it is, he may
drop around to see you, but he'll be a lot more considerate
in asking questions than any cop is accustomed to being.''

"You mentioned nothing about the—ah—matter of
major interest?''

That would be the manuscript. ''No, sir. If you don't
mind a suggestion, I see no reason for you to mention
it, either. Not unless you're satisfied to have the story
spread all over the Sunday supplements.''

I could almost feel his shudder over the telephone wire.
"That mustn't happen,'' he said sharply. "I must insist
you keep confidential everything I told you on that sub-
ject.''

"You can depend on it.''

His voice softened slightly. "Do the police think Wirtz
murdered this man Post? That is, it is murder, isn't it?
From what you've told me . . .''

"You bet it's murder. With a knife and very messy.

They seem to think so, all right. The fact the killing took place in his room, plus his being missing, kind of piles it up against him."

"Your own opinion?"

"I have no opinion. Yet. I'll try to get one if you wish."

"Find him, Mr. Pine." His voice sounded curiously flat. "He's a troubled man; a disillusioned man. But he seems too—well—too academic to kill a man with a knife. That way. He should have somebody on his side, at least until all the facts come out.

"Besides—" he cleared his throat—"the manuscript. As you know, it has fired my imagination until I can think of little else. If there should be such a document——"

"I'll be in there swinging," I said soothingly.

"Please keep me informed."

"I'll do that."

He said good-by, his voice a little unsteady, and I laid the receiver gently back in its cradle and reached for the stub of my cigarette. I finished it and most of another before I could dig up an idea that might do me some good.

The phone again. I dictated a lengthy telegram to Western Union, addressed to Cliff Morrison, a wine-drinking, woman-chasing friend of mine who had worked for several of the private agencies around town before moving to Los Angeles and starting an agency of his own. He was getting rich—not off the movie colony either—and for the past two years had been after me to come out there and work for him. But I had steadfastly refused on the grounds that I was afraid of being brained by a falling orange.

One more avenue left to follow. The phone book gave me the number. Two buzzes came over the wire, then one of those disinterested female voices you find behind all switchboards said, "Stevens Hotel."

"Room 2212," I said.

A click for the plug going in, three more quick ones for a key being waggled . . .

"Yeah?"

A man's voice. I saw him as a man of beef and thinning hair and clothing cut to hide a paunch. A man who spent a lot of time in barber chairs, who dated the manicurist and was strong for girlie shows. A man who had been out all morning peddling cosmetics or concrete mixers or corrugated boxes and who was getting ready to step under a shower.

I said, "Is this 2212?

"Yeah, that's right." Impatient now. "Who'd you want?"

"I understood a Miss North had this room."

"No such luck, brother! Haw, haw! I just now come in here and not a woman in the place. Course I ain't looked in the bed yet, but——"

I pressed the cut-off bar, then called the Stevens again. Miss North, I was told, had checked out less than an hour before, leaving no forwarding address. I asked for the permanent address shown on her registration card and got snooted by an assistant manager until I thought up a story plausible enough to learn she had put down only New York City. People do that when they think such information is none of the hotel's business.

It seemed I had muffed one by not hanging onto Lola North until I chiseled a few facts out of her. It was just that I hadn't known about the corpse in the closet while she was still with me. That, I reflected gloomily, was my fault too.

Well, she was gone now, gone completely, and nothing I could do about it. If she was interested in the manuscript Wirtz was supposed to have I might run into her again. It was a possibility, however faint. But now my only real remaining hope of a lead on Raymond Wirtz depended on Cliff Morrison's answer to my wire. That might be days away.

Interviewing a client, finding a body, sparring with

the law and losing a nicely filled pair of nylons seemed enough work for one day. I got out of the chair, closed the window and took my hat off the filing cabinet. There was a movie at the Apollo about a private eye that should be good for laughs. I could certainly use a few.

The phone bell stopped me as I was opening the corridor door. I went back, unlocked the inner door again and picked up the receiver.

"Mr. Pine?" A man's voice, young and crisp and self-confident, against background noises of typewriters and loud conversation.

"Uh-hunh."

"My name is Grant, Mr. Pine. With the *Herald-American*. We're informed you were the one who found Willie Post's body out at that Erie Street address this morning."

"Who gave you that?"

He must have caught the annoyance in my voice; it was there to catch. He sounded a little apologetic. "One of the police officers on the case."

That would be the young cop with the leading-man profile. Any cop who went around leaning on his siren when there was no need for it would spell his name and spill his guts on the first leg man who showed up.

I said, "What's on your mind?"

He turned on a brand of persuasive charm. "Simply a matter of getting the facts straight. We wouldn't want to say anything you might object to. Naturally. That's why we'd like your own version of how you happened to find the body."

"I was looking for the bathroom," I said, "and got my directions mixed."

His polite laugh was as hard and humorless as a tombstone. "Well now, Mr. Pine, I'm sure you can do better than that. We understand the police are looking for this man Walsh, whose room Post was found in. Who is he? Where's he from? What did he have to do with Willie Post?"

"Who's Walsh?" I said. "I never heard of him."

There was a pause. Then: "I do wish you'd be more co-operative, Mr. Pine." Mr. Grant was hurt and a little offended in a gentlemanly way. "Try to understand *our* position. Besides, a man in your line might need some help from us occasionally."

"Sorry," I said, "but I give all my business to the *News*."

I hung up on him and left the office. While on my way down the hall I heard the telephone start up again. I left it ringing and went on to the elevators.

# · 5 ·

The corner clock said four-seventeen when I came out of the theater. I stood there and blinked at the strong sunlight filling Randolph Street and thought about going back to the office for an hour or two before dinner. There was no reason to go back actually. I had a case but it was at a dead end and would probably stay there until I got an answer to the wire I had sent Cliff Morrison.

There was a phone number or two in my address book, either of which could keep the evening from being a total loss. But there was a novel by Philip Wylie on the night table next to my bed and there were Scotch and seltzer in the kitchen. . . .

Off to the east gray clouds, so dark they were almost black, were piling up out over the lake and the slight breeze was noticeably cooler. It appeared we were going to be in for some rain, and not very long before it arrived, either. That made the thought of my own apartment the best one of the day.

But suddenly I realized I was no longer interested in that novel on my bedside table. I wanted soft lights and glasses filled with amber liquid and warm curves in a party dress across from me at a secluded table. This had been a day filled with the wrong kind of people, largely. An antidote was indicated, and thanks to Bishop McManus I could afford to fill the prescription.

I scooped a late edition of the *Herald-American* off the corner newsstand, got into a cab and gave my office address—where I kept my list of phone numbers—then leaned back and unfolded the paper. The headline that had caught my eye read: FIND ANTUNI AIDE SLAIN.

The left-hand column had the story, under bold black subheads. I read it through with that slightly pleasant feeling of being part of the news.

> The body of Vito Postori, alias Willie Post, onetime lieutenant and alleged triggerman for the once-powerful Antuni syndicate, was today found in a rooming house at 1730 West Erie. Death had resulted from a knife wound below the heart. According to a coroner's report, Post had been dead for several days. Discovery of the crime was made by Paul Pine, a private detective, whose presence at the scene has so far not been explained.
>
> Mrs. Agnes Trotter, owner and operator of the rooming house at the Erie Street address, reported that the room in which Post was found had been rented two weeks before by a Raymond Walsh. Walsh is said to have been missing for the past several days, although his personal belongings were still in the room. Police are searching for him.

The balance of the article told of Post's disappearance from the Chicago scene nearly thirteen years before, explaining that it was no secret that he, along with other of Antuni's boys, had joined the Big Guy in Florida after the latter's release from the Federal penitentiary on California's Terminal Island. The last line of the piece mentioned what was common knowledge: Louis Antuni was suffering from an "incurable" disease and his sands were about to run out.

A drizzle was falling by the time I got out of the cab in front of the Clawson Building and people were huddled in the entrance, looking forlornly at the sky. I pushed through into the lobby and rode up to the eighth floor.

My reception room was dim and shadowy in the gray half-light from the window. I got out my keys, turned the right one in the lock on the inner door and was two steps over the threshold before I realized the door hadn't been locked at all.

That couldn't be right. I had locked it. I always locked it. A careful guy like me.

Whoever was behind the blackjack must have been an old hand at the game. I never heard a thing.

It was one of those dinky hunks of ribbon women call hats. This one was blue and there was a smooth triangle of shiny silver cloth to hold the ends together. What there was of it was set at a fetching angle on smooth red hair.

Both hair and hat faded and came back and faded again. Then they spun sideways in a breath-taking swoop like a falling elevator . . . and I shut my eyes and clamped my lips to keep from committing a nuisance.

Bells, great golden-toned bells, pealed out their notes in an empty echoing hall twelve miles wide and sixty miles long. I shook with the sound and wondered why there was no light.

And then there was light—too much of it and too bright, and the clang of bells became words:

". . . Open your eyes? Are you all right? Can you hear me?"

I got a shoulder under my eyelids and heaved hard and they slid up about halfway before they stuck again. It was like opening cottage windows after a rain. Pain gnawed at the back of my head like rats in a granary.

The hunk of ribbon and the smooth red hair were back again, with a face under them I hadn't noticed before.

It was a face to bring hermits down out of the hills, to fill divorce courts, to make old men read up on hormones. A face that could sell perfume or black lace

undies and make kitchen aprons a drug on the market.
Good skin under expert make-up to make it look even
better. Brown eyes, with a silken sheen to them. Eyes
with a careful, still look as though never just sure what
the brain behind them was up to. A nose you never quite
saw because her full lips kept pulling you away from it.
Hair smooth on top and a medium bob in back that was
pushed up here and there to make it casually terrific.

And my aching head was supported pleasantly on a
cloth-covered length of firm warm flesh that was one of
the lady's thighs.

I said, "I laughed at a scene like this not more than
an hour ago. I thought the usher was going to throw me
out."

Her expression said she thought I was out of my head.
I would have liked to be, after what had been done to
it.

"Are you all right?" It was the kind of voice the rest
of her deserved: husky, full-throated, yet subdued.

I said, "How do I know if I'm all right? I think I'll
kind of stand up."

She helped me into a sitting position and I sat there
and stared at the section of linoleum between my legs
until my head stopped spinning. Then I clawed my way
up the side of my desk, hung there for another minute
before weaving my way to the swivel chair. Sitting down
helped. Not as much as two weeks in Hot Springs would
have, but some. I blinked at the confusion of papers,
matchbook folders, blotters and rubber bands littering
the floor in a broad semicircle behind the desk.

My visitor stood across from me, half-smiling to help
my morale but concerned a little, too. "How do you
feel, Mr. Pine?"

"Adequate," I said. "Thanks for being patient. I'm
awake now and reasonably alert. Were you the one who
sapped me?"

"Certainly not! I came in just a few moments ago and
found you on the floor and things strewed around."

"I see." The ceiling light was on and the Venetian blind was down and closed. Neither had been that way when I walked out earlier that afternoon. A ladies' green-and-white-checked umbrella, closed, stood handle up in the corner nearest the open door. It didn't appear to have hit any heads lately.

She was eying me curiously, just the hint of a smile tugging at the corners of her mouth. "Aren't you going to make sure nothing of value is missing?"

"I never had anything of value. Won't you sit down?"

She laughed musically. "You seem to be an unusual person, Mr. Pine. Thank you; I will sit down."

She moved the customer's chair into position alongside the desk, sat in it and crossed not quite slender legs in black nylons. I never did notice her shoes. She was wearing a dark-blue sheer wool dress, very simple in the lines and very flattering to a figure that was going to be voluptuous in a few years. The neckline was rounded and not too high and the skin above it was as clear as a saint's conscience.

A lot of money had gone into cutting her age from a good thirty-five to an excellent twenty-eight. Money, I judged, was where she could reach it any old time.

I looked at the blue alligator bag in her lap, at the rings on her fingers, at the single strand of pearls at her neck. I looked at the telephone, at my fingers, at nothing at all. I was going home and put my head under a cold shower as soon as possible.

"I'm Constance Benbrook, Mr. Pine. Don't you think it would be wise to see a doctor? You may have a concussion."

I got out my cigarettes, offered her one, had it refused. I sat there and stared at the cigarette's tailored orderly smoothness until I was sure my eyes were focusing correctly. Sometimes a hit on the head throws them off.

All clear. I found a match and got the tobacco burning. The first lungful of smoke seemed to help. I looked up to find her brown eyes worrying over me.

"How do you do, Mrs. Benbrook. No, I don't need a doctor."

She lifted one delicately curved eyebrow. "You've impressed me already! How did you know it was *Mrs.* Benbrook?"

"You're wearing a wedding ring. From here it looks like one made to order by Peacock's. That means you're married and very rich. Elementary, Mrs. Benbrook. What can I do for you?"

She laughed. Pleasantly, sincerely and without throwing her head back to do it. "A woman gets so used to wearing one. . . . I want you to find my husband, Mr. Pine."

I breathed in some more smoke and shook my head. "I'm sorry, Mrs. Benbrook. I'm a one-man agency and, because of that, can handle only one client at a time. Not enough work comes in for me to build up a staff."

"You're working on a case at the present time?"

"That's right."

She hesitated, drew her lower lip between her teeth before letting it slip slowly free again. "I'm not sure . . ." She stopped there to rearrange the way she was going to say it. "The fact that my husband is missing may have something to do with your present assignment."

The words seemed to hang in the air between us. It was the last thing in the world I would have expected her to say and I had a job keeping my thoughts off my face.

After a moment I said, "I'd like to hear a little more, Mrs. Benbrook. Even if it's nothing I can use, I won't go around repeating it."

Her ungloved hands moved restlessly in her lap, stroking the surface of her bag as though she liked to touch expensive things. She said, "I saw your name in the paper earlier this afternoon—in connection with a man named Walsh."

"Uh-hunh," I said encouragingly, when she hesitated.

"His real name is Wirtz, Mr. Pine. He's an old friend

of my husband. Myles was on the board of a museum here in town for years and Wirtz did some work for the museum on several occasions.''

I said, "By Myles you mean your husband?"

"Yes. Myles Benbrook. We were married three years ago—I'm his second wife and quite a bit younger than he—and spent our honeymoon in California. We saw quite a bit of Raymond Wirtz out there.

"Then about two weeks ago he showed up at the house. Said he'd just driven in from California and was here on something awfully important, that he had taken a cheap room and would be here for ten days or so. We hardly recognized him, Mr. Pine. He looked actually haggard, and so nervous and jumpy he just couldn't sit still. He seemed to have added ten years to his age since we had last seen him."

"How old a man is he, actually?"

"Well, Myles is forty-seven and Mr. Wirtz must be about the same age."

"He have a wife?"

"Yes. Although I've never met her. He married a younger woman a couple of years ago. It didn't last very long, I understand."

"Divorced?"

She thought about it, trying to remember. She looked lovely just thinking. "Separated, I believe. I'm really not sure."

I flicked cigarette ashes on the floor to join the mess already there. "Let's hear the rest of it, Mrs. Benbrook. If you don't mind."

Those large brown eyes were being wistfully hopeful now. "You're going to help me, Mr. Pine?"

"We'll see. I think so."

She hit me with a smile I felt all the way to my knees. "I'm so glad. I've been so worried about Myles."

I said, getting down to business, "Did Wirtz give you any details on this important matter he mentioned?"

"Not that I heard. But Myles and he spent almost two

hours locked in the library that same afternoon. When they came out and Mr. Wirtz had left, Myles was terribly excited about something—he wouldn't tell me what. I didn't see Mr. Wirtz again, although I know he called Myles several times in the next few days. I don't know what they talked about, but daily Myles seemed to become more and more nervous and—and irritable. Actually I saw very little of Myles from the time Mr. Wirtz arrived until he—my husband—disappeared entirely."

"How long ago did he disappear?"

"Three days ago."

"They know anything at his office?"

"Myles has no office, Mr. Pine. He retired from business over three years ago. He had been a broker on La Salle Street until then, but only to keep himself occupied. You see, his father left him a great deal of money."

I got out of my chair, drew up the blind halfway and tugged open the lower section of window a few inches. Rain, steady but not especially heavy, fell straight down from a sky that seemed completely overcast now. I leaned my head against the window glass, grateful for the coolness, and some of the bees stopped buzzing in my skull.

"Are you all right, Mr. Pine?" A little worried, a little impatient, even a little seductive. That last surprised me into turning around.

She was smiling, not much but enough to show a white line that was the edge of her upper teeth, and there was frank approval of me in her eyes. I wondered fuzzily what I had done to earn it.

I came back and sat down again. My legs were steadier and my head had become something I could get along with. A drink would have completed the cure, but I no longer kept a bottle in the bottom drawer of my desk. The private-eye movies had made me self-conscious about it.

"Three days isn't very long, Mrs. Benbrook. Any other reason why he might leave you? Granting, of course, that one reason might be this Wirtz matter."

She crossed her legs the other way, hiking the wool skirt up more than even rank carelessness should have managed. I could see a triangular portion of creamy skin above the top of one stocking. She made no effort to do anything about it.

"It's rather awkward to put into words," she said slowly. While hunting for the words, she opened her purse and took out cigarettes and a gold-ribbed lighter with her initials in platinum inlay on one side. Even the cigarette, oval, king-sized and straw-tipped, looked expensive. She lighted it before I could find my matches, and blew out a white plume of smoke. "There may be another woman. I can't understand why."

I couldn't either, just by looking at her. "Tell me about it."

"About noon of the day Myles disappeared he was speaking with a woman on the telephone in the library. I happened to pick up an upstairs extension and heard her say, 'Don't even tell her. You'd better make it after dark.' Myles evidently had heard the extension receiver go up, for he said, 'Good-by' immediately and hung up."

"Did this woman hang up right away?"

"No. Myles must have caught her by surprise. She said, 'Hello' very quickly a time or two. I cut in and said, 'I'm afraid my husband isn't on the wire. May I have him call you back?' "

"Uh-hunh," I said admiringly. "That let her know she had been talking to a married man. Did she answer you?"

"No. She put the receiver down at her end very softly."

"Did you try to trace the call?"

She laughed shortly. "I wouldn't have the slightest idea how to go about such a thing."

"You mention this to your husband?"

"No. I didn't know enough to make it worth-while bringing up. I would have had to be content with whatever explanation he gave."

I stroked the back of my head tenderly and made a half-hearted effort to keep my eyes off the rounded neckline of her dress. "Are you in love with your husband, Mrs. Benbrook?"

"Aren't you being insolent, Mr. Pine?" Cool but not angry, even faintly amused.

"How true. Forgive me. Are you?"

"My husband is a wonderful man. He is also not a young man." The still, careful look was back in her eyes and stronger than ever.

I said, "I wouldn't call forty-seven old."

She dropped ashes from her cigarette into the glass tray I had put on the desk where she could reach it. Her hand looked strong and capable for all its too long, too red nails. "A man can be much older than his years in some ways, Mr. Pine. A woman doesn't like that." A ghost's ghost of a smile moved along her full-lipped warm mouth. "Not my kind of woman. But money is important—to my kind of woman."

I didn't say anything. My head ached and my mouth tasted like a vulture roost. Rain whispered against the window and a wet dusk was settling down over the upper reaches of Jackson Boulevard. It was time for me to go home. Constance Benbrook was a beautiful woman whose glands were stronger than her inhibitions. Shake the tree even gently and she'd fall right in your lap. Only I didn't want her in my lap right then. Maybe some other day.

"You'll find him for me, Mr. Pine?"

I shrugged. "Possibly. I'll try. You've given me hardly anything to go on, though. Maybe a list of his closer friends and a few business acquaintances. Suppose I stop by at your place some time tomorrow and pick it up. If you don't mind. Right now I'm a little fed up with my kind of job."

"Of course." Sympathetic and exciting at the same time. Not easy, even for a woman as beautiful as Constance Benbrook. "The address is 6174 Sheridan Road."

I wrote it down while she stood up and smoothed her dress. "The afternoon some time? Say about two-thirty?"

"Two-thirty will be fine," I said.

She picked up her umbrella before I could get over to do it for her, and was on the way out when she remembered I probably worked for money. I told her we could go into that the next day and she said good-by and gave me a lingering smile and went away, leaving against the smell of wet plaster the subtle scent of an expensive perfume to remember her by.

I closed the window and stood there looking at the rows of lighted windows in the office building across from me while I thumbed through my thoughts. At noon, Lola North and her .25-caliber Colt automatic; at five o'clock Constance Benbrook and her sex appeal—if they still called it that.

Myles Benbrook was a friend of Raymond Wirtz. Benbrook had disappeared three days ago after getting a phone call from a woman. Lola North was a woman and also interested in Raymond Wirtz. A connection? Three days ago Raymond Wirtz, alias Walsh, had walked out of the office of Bishop McManus and hadn't been seen since. The corpse of a retired hoodlum had been found in Wirtz's closet. It might well have been put there three days ago.

A connection? There's one laying around some place. Pine will find it. Pine can find anything. Pine can find your husband or your dog or strawberries out of season. Pine can find a blackjack, if you lay it against his skull.

Nuts.

I sneered at my reflection in the glass, took my hat off the linoleum and reshaped it, scowled at the mess on the floor behind the desk, turned out the light and got out of there. It was a pleasure.

# ·6·

A squat and cheerful Negro hustler brought down my Plymouth. He flashed his teeth at me, said, "Evenin', Mistuh Pine. Wet out, ain't it?" and opened the car door. Light from a neon sign over the cashier's cage gave a red cast to his ebony features.

"We must be thankful," I said, "because it's good for the crops. Also it takes the curl out of your hair and puts it in your pants legs. You can have it."

"Yassuh."

The combination of wet streets and the evening rush hour made reaching Pratt Boulevard on Chicago's North Side, an hour's job. I stretched that into an hour and a half by stopping off at a neighborhood restaurant for a light dinner, before driving on and parking on Wayne Avenue, half a block south of the Dinsmore Arms where I kept two rooms and a kitchenette.

I locked the car and sprinted along the deserted walk to the Dinsmore. There were quite a number of my neighbors hanging around the softly lighted lobby waiting for the rain to let up. I crossed to the desk to get my mail and phone messages, if any.

It was too early for Sam Wilson, the pulp-magazine-reading night man, to be on duty, and the correct young man on the day shift had looked down his nose at me too often to waste my time on. He said there was no mail and no messages and his tone said I had a hell of a nerve for making him look. He might have been right.

I rode up in the self-service elevator with the blonde librarian who had taken the apartment across the hall from me a week or so before. It could have worked into a date, but she had a copy of Dante's *Inferno* under one arm and I figured I couldn't show her a time half so hot as that. After she closed her door I unlocked mine and went in and flicked on the light switch.

The two table lamps flanking the couch threw a soft restrained glow through the living room. I stood there with my finger still on the switch and blinked at two men coming through the swinging door that closed off the kitchenette from the rest of the apartment.

Both of them wore raincoats and moisture gleamed on sleeves and shoulders. One was tall and much too thin, with a long disagreeable face and small, hard gray eyes set close to a thin nose that had been broken once and set by a bootblack. The other man was of standard size, older than the first and he didn't look as though he got around very well. But his face was hard and more intelligent-looking than that of his companion . . . and he was the one with the gun.

I looked at the gun. It was a nickel-plated Bankers' Special with the sight filed away and it was pointed at me. I said, "I keep my money in the bank and my jewels in a hock shop. Why not try the guy next door?"

"Save the gags, Mac," the thin one said. "And take that hand off the switch before you make a mistake."

I lowered my hand. He walked around behind me, his feet soundless on my sand-colored carpet, and slid his hands lightly along my sides, patted my pockets and belt line. He forgot to feel around my knees for a stiletto but that was all right. I didn't have a stiletto. He said, "No rod," across my shoulder to the other man, his breath warm against my cheek and heavy with the smell of beer. I could have reached back and clamped a headlock on him and used him for a shield. I could have gone over Niagara in an orange crate, too.

He came around in front of me and took hold of my coat lapel with a square hand that had black swirls of hair across its back and along the fingers.

"Nothing personal, Mac," he said in a soft voice. "You look like a nice smart lad who knows the score and hates trouble. We want your company for a while is all. On a little trip."

I looked from him to the man with the gun. "You can do better than that," I said. "What's the general idea?"

The hand holding my lapel jerked a little. Nothing rough, just enough to show who was doing the talking. The soft voice said, "I guess you better put on a raincoat, hunh? No sense getting rained on. Where would it be, Mac?"

"Bedroom closet," I said. "No hurry. Let's talk about this over a drink or two."

He dropped his hand from my coat, turned and walked on cat feet into the bedroom. He was back almost at once, my trench coat trailing from one hand. He felt in the pockets, then tossed the garment to me, his expression still friendly in a distant manner.

"Get into it," he said.

I put it on, my fingers stiff on the buttons. The old guy tucked the gun in a side pocket of his raincoat, leaving his hand in to keep it company. He tilted his head at the corridor door and we started toward it.

Knuckles rapped lightly on the opposite side.

The sound froze all three of us. The thin man, indecision marking his face, looked from the door to me and back at the door again. His companion took the Bankers' Special very quickly from his pocket and held it along his side, the barrel pointing at the floor.

This time the buzzer sounded.

I said, keeping my voice low, "The light shows under the door. That means I'm home, so my friend won't leave easy, and I don't have a back door. Any remarks?"

The thin guy made up his mind. "Put it away,

Whitey," he said to the man with the gun, then, to me: "We're going out. Tell your friend to come back later. And tell it the right way or earn yourself a slug. I mean it, Mac."

I shrugged. "Whatever you say."

His long arm shot out, twisted the knob and drew open the door.

Lola North was standing there, in the act of reaching for the buzzer again. At sight of the three of us her mouth unhinged slightly and she stepped back. She said very rapidly, "I'm sorry, Mr. Pine. I didn't know you were— busy. Shall I come back later?"

I smiled at her like a man without a care in the world. "Was it something urgent, Miss North? I can't say exactly when I'll be here."

She was wearing one of those reversible spring coats with the waterproof side out. Her blonde head was bare and raindrops sparkled along the strands like brilliants on gold wire. The high neckline of a yellow blouse showed between the open lapels of her coat. She looked lovely and cool and very, very intense about something.

"It can wait," she said reluctantly. "Of course. Perhaps tomorrow morning . . ."

She ran down like a dollar watch on that last word. Her eyes were suddenly fastened on the right-hand pocket of the man called Whitey, where his hand bulged against the material. Outlined in cloth was the unmistakable shape of a gun barrel, pointed at my liver. Her expression said my liver meant a great deal to her.

The thin guy caught on immediately. His hand made an eagle's swoop and caught one of Lola North's wrists and jerked her through the door and had it closed before she could protest.

He leaned against the wall and moved his eyes slowly over her. "You picked a bad time, sister."

"I—I don't understand," she said faintly. "I only dropped in to talk to Mr. Pine about something. I . . ."

That was all. She had gone as far as she could. Now it was up to him.

The thin guy said, "You're all right, lady. Relax. You kind of butted in on something. Maybe you won't mind being tied up a little. Just so you won't do any quick yelling."

I said, "I heard of a case once. Girl got tied and gagged and she suffocated. The State called it murder."

He said, "Shut up," absently and continued to look at the girl while he scratched his ear with slow care. Then: "Guess maybe you better come along, honey. Seems the best way."

"I won't go!"

"Sure you'll go." He shifted his slate-gray eyes to the other man. "A sound out of either of 'em, Whitey, and give it to the broad. Let's go."

Nobody was in the corridor and the only sounds came from behind other doors along the way. Small domestic sounds: a radio playing dinner music, a woman's voice shrill with anger, the muted buzz of an electric razor. The ordinary sounds made by ordinary people who were smart enough to make their living in a world where guns were pointed by and at only the unsmart kind of people.

"The back stairs, Mac," the thin guy said quietly. "We meet anybody, don't make no fuss."

They walked behind us down the two flights of bare concrete, our steps loud against the silence. We came out on the first floor, well down from the elevator and a long way back from the desk. Ceiling lights, recessed, cast a pale amber glow along the corridor and glinted on the door numbers.

"The back way out," the thin one said in his normal voice.

I led them to the corridor's end and dragged open the heavy door. We came out into a narrow cemented-over areaway lighted by a sealed beam flood lamp. Lola North and I led the parade along a narrow runway to a paved alley, lined with giant-size garbage cans, along this to the street. The rain was coming down heavily now and I turned the collar of my trench coat against it.

We were out on Wayne Avenue now, a few doors south of the Dinsmore. A car rolled slowly past our tight little group, its tires whispering on the wet asphalt, raindrops appearing large and plentiful in the golden lances of the headlights.

"We'll use your scooter, Mac," the soft voice said in my ear. "Where's she parked?"

I told him, the words thick in my ears, and we went along the walk to the Plymouth. I wondered how they knew I had a car, but it didn't seem important enough to ask about. I probably wouldn't get an answer anyway.

I found my keys and unlocked the right-hand door. The old guy tilted the front seat and indicated that Miss North would find the rear seat quite comfortable. She pushed in, her movements as relaxed as any puppet's, and he followed her. He did so slowly, as though bending wasn't so easy for him any more.

On orders, I slid in behind the wheel and the thin man got in beside me and drew the door shut.

"Roll her, Mac."

I unlocked the ignition before giving it one last try. "Fun," I said, "is fun and I've always said so. But just for the record and my peace of mind, for whatever that's worth, what's behind this hard-eye and ready-gun routine?"

The man beside me shifted his left foot and pressed the starter and the motor began to throb. He said pleasantly, "Not now, Mac. We don't want to keep these nice people waiting. Move her."

"Yeah. Do I just drive around the block or would you like to suggest something?" My tone told him how I felt about it.

A lot he cared how I felt. "Get over to Western and take it south."

I made a U turn and drove back to Pratt Boulevard, then west toward Western. My strap watch said it was a few minutes past seven but the sky was already empty of daylight.

The streets out there were lined mostly with large and fairly new apartment buildings, with an occasional private home, spacious and substantial behind a hedge, to break the monotony. Massive cottonwoods and elms hung over walks, parkways and gutters to create dank tunnels filled with shifting shadows and the formless bulk of parked cars.

Rain hammered steadily on the car roof and at the windows, clouding the glass and sealing us in. There was a smell of damp cloth and a suggestion of perspiration, and there were the small noises people make when they're just sitting.

The blocks swept by. Light from intersection lamps winked in and out of the car's interior, the motor hummed quietly to itself, the windshield wipers went *swish-ah*, *swish-ah*, the old guy behind me breathed asthmatically.

Western Avenue, well lighted, very wide and with streetcar tracks down its center, loomed ahead. I swung south into it, keeping the needle at thirty-five. There was considerably more traffic here and I kept my thoughts hard on my driving.

Shortly after we passed Wilson Avenue, the thin man came to life. "West on Irving, Mac."

"Very good, sir."

Irving Park was another streetcar line and the Plymouth bounced some along the bricks as I swung into it. The miles fell back and the rain went on and traffic lights gleamed red, amber and green.

Out near the western edge of town my seatmate began to squirm around, trying to catch a glimpse of the intersection street markers. I slowed at his order and a little later he said, "Left at the next corner. Third house on the east side of the street."

"Aye, aye, sir."

He grunted with what might have been amusement but probably wasn't. I made the turn, rolled on the required distance and swung into the curb and applied my brakes in front of a small brick bungalow lost in heavy shadows from two huge sycamores flanking the walk. A fifty-foot lawn and two hedges kept at bay the neighbors on either side.

The four of us got out and went along a walk that curved for no reason, under the dripping limbs of the sycamores and up onto a small porch. The man with the vocal cords put his thumb against a white button and a buzzer gave a bronx cheer from inside. The door moved back three inches on a chain and a grumpy voice from the darkness beyond said, "Yeah?" in a voice that hinted bullets would start flying if the password wasn't right.

"Riley," the thin one said. "Open the goddam door."

It closed far enough to release the chain, then swung all the way back. We went into what I suspected was a hall, although it was as dark as the inside of a cannibal. The blackness lasted until the door was shut and the chain fumbled back into place. It seemed an awful lot of precaution.

A switch clicked and I blinked at a narrow hall with an oak trim and green-and-white-striped paper on the walls.

Three men now, the new one short and stocky in gray trousers and a white shirt open at the neck. He was well along in years but still husky enough to give you trouble. He would love to give you trouble, his expression said. Any time and any place. He looked at me out of a lumpy face, then at Lola North. A tired leer tried to crawl into his eyes at sight of her but gave up from lack of practice, and his gaze came back to me again. I got a sneer instead of a leer.

"This is the gee, hunh? Pretty boy for a shamus. They must be teaching it in college these days."

I said, "Your job was to open the door, grandpa. Now you can get back to your broom."

His yellow-gray eyes turned opaque as paint. He said tightly, "Why, you lousy elbow!" and swung the toe of a pointed shoe at my shin.

I moved my leg quick enough to make him miss, then put a palm against his shirt front and shoved. He slammed into the wall hard enough to shake it, banging his head smartly and leaving an oil stain on the paper. He stood there, panting shallowly, his eyes vacant with shock and his knees unsteady.

The thin one, Riley, appeared faintly amused. "Shame on you. An old man like that." He indicated a closed door at the far end of the hall. "Down there, Pine. You too, honey."

The man with the gun in his pocket followed us back there. Riley bent the fingers of his right hand and tapped the knuckles lightly against the white-enameled panel.

"Who is it?" A woman's voice, hard and brassy as a cartridge shell.

"Riley. We got the guy."

"Come on in."

It was a bedroom turned sitting room and office by removing the bed and substituting a handsome walnut desk complete with glass top, telephone and a fluorescent lamp with a copper standard the color of a new penny. There was a modern couch against a side wall, two lounge chairs in contrasting solid colors, a green and brown rug and a walnut liquor cabinet almost the size of the desk. All new and shiny as if the delivery truck were just pulling out of the driveway. Ivory-metal Venetian blinds were lowered and tightly closed, but not any more tightly closed than the two windows beyond them. Heat from a radiator hissing softly in one corner made the air humid as the steamroom of a Turkish bath. There was light, plenty of light, but I couldn't tell exactly where it was coming from.

A room done without much imagination but nothing about it to make you shudder.

A tall blonde, with a hard empty face, a slinky red evening gown pulled much too tightly around a better than average figure, was on the couch with her feet drawn under her and a highball glass in one hand. She regarded me with complete disinterest as I came in with Lola and the boys.

But the man in the chair behind the desk was worth more than a second glance. He wore a heavy dark suit, complete with buttoned vest, and a wool dressing robe in figured brown over that. Such an outfit, with the outdoor temperature in the seventies and the corner radiator going full blast, would have melted down a monument. Beads of moisture dotted the sallow waxlike skin of his forehead and cheeks but he seemed chilled to the bone.

He sat there, arms hugging his chest, and looked at me out of a face that was old and haggard and lined with suffering. Only a pair of brown eyes that seemed much too large for his face, and his neatly combed curly black hair, had the sheen of life to them.

I recognized him, but only because his name had come up several times during the past twelve hours.

Louis Antuni. The Mr. Big of Prohibition days in Chicago. Louie Antuni, referred to also as the Big Guy, the open-handed, suave, cheerful Sicilian of the Roaring Twenties. The king of alky cookers, the prince of horse parlors, the potentate of pimps, the nabob of numbers. The man who handed out diamond-studded tie clasps and bronze-bound caskets, often to the same men. The man who was responsible for more deaths than many, but who had kissed off all raps except for the one the man with the star-spangled hat hung on him for income tax evasion. That had taken him out of the game, and he stayed out even after the doors of the Big House opened for him nearly four years later.

It all seemed a long time ago.

Only this wasn't the Louie Antuni of the old days. Not by eleven thousand miles it wasn't. This was an old man, a sick man, a man who was breathing and whose breathing took all his determination and most of his strength.

His eyes stayed on me—emotionless, expressionless, empty of everything except life—until they would know me from this day forward. It was impossible to look into those eyes for very long. I felt a trickle of perspiration along the skin of my chest. The room was hot but I hadn't realized it was that hot. . . .

He shifted his gaze to Lola North—Lola with her golden hair glinting under the indirect lighting, the hollows under her cheekbones strangely accentuated, her expression a kind of propped-up haughtiness which the fear in her blue-black eyes denied. . . .

She took that obsidian stare for all of five seconds, then the color rushed into her face and the muscles of her throat moved spasmodically. She looked down at the tips of her shoes and one hand reached out blindly and caught my arm.

Nothing changed in Antuni's face. A thick tongue, so gray it seemed more nearly white, came out slowly and touched shrunken lips. He took two deep breaths to get his voice up on its feet, and said, "What ees thees, Riley? I say breeng Meester Pine. Who ees thees woman?"

His voice was even more of a shock than his appearance. It was harsh, whispering, like sandpaper against mortar. The cords of his wasted neck twitched and crawled with strain. Right then is when I first became aware of an odor of corruption in the room—the reek of malignancy.

Riley, who had been examining a line in the palm of his left hand, looked at the man behind the desk with casual solemnity. "She was with him, Louie. Leaving her could of been a mistake."

"Take her out."

"Come on, honey."

She looked at me in silent appeal and fear was suddenly strong in every line of her. I said, "She belongs with me, Antuni. Let her stay."

Yellow talons that once must have been fingers came down and fastened themselves to the arms of his chair. "You know me, hah, Meester Pine?"

"Uh-hunh."

"Not much like the old Louie, no?" There might have been bitterness in his tone. I couldn't tell.

"I wouldn't know about that," I said.

"Thees young lady she'sa wait een the nex' room. I wan' a private talk, Meester Pine."

I shook my head. "Not with the kind of boys you got out there. Besides I tell her everything."

He shrugged to show I could have my own way—at least on that point. He went through another of his breathing exercises, then said, "You know why you are here, Meester Pine?"

"Certainly I know. A Bankers' Special came and got me."

"You don' like thees, hah?"

"Would it make a difference?"

Flames seemed to move in the brown depths of his eyes. "Don' get wise weeth me, you son va beetch."

The gloves were off. Now I knew where I stood. Why I stood there was something I knew nothing about and I might be dead and the concrete mixed for my feet without ever learning the answer.

For a long moment Antuni studied me from under sagging eyelids, then he jerked his head at the two men and they went out as quickly and as quietly as candle flames. In the silence the blonde clicked a fingernail against her glass and looked increasingly bored.

Abruptly he leaned forward and burned me with his gaze. "How much he'sa pay you, Meester Pine?"

"How much is who paying me?"

"Thees Jafar Baijan ees who. Tell me."

"I don't know anyone by that name, Mr. Antuni."

He thought about my answer for a long time. Finally he leaned back in his chair and drew the tips of his fingers across his forehead in a gesture that was infinitely weary and somehow pathetic.

He said, "I am tired and eet ees hard for me to talk much. I don' wan' you to tell me lies. The paper she'sa say you fin' Vito. I wan' to know about thees."

I said, "Any objection to our sitting down?"

He hadn't thought of that. He waved a hand at the easy chairs. Even that seemed an effort for him. I helped Miss North out of her raincoat shrugged out of mine and laid both of them across one arm of the couch. I sat down in the other chair, put my hat on the floor and looked thirstily at the glass in the blonde's hand. She sucked at her drink and memorized the lobe of my left ear.

Antuni's harsh whisper reached me. "Well, Meester Pine."

I showed him a countenance as open and frank as a Boy Scout's. "I'm not too proud to admit I haven't the slightest idea why you sent for me, Mr. Antuni. You knew my name and you knew where to find me. That means you know what business I'm in, as well.

"Right now I'm working on a case. If that case has any connection with you or with any of your boys, I didn't know it when I took the job and I don't know it now. I was sent out to that Erie Street address to see a man named Walsh. He was out. In looking around I found a body hanging in the closet. I didn't know whose body it was until the police told me. He was dead when I found him, and if I'm any judge he was dead before I was hired. That's the whole story and it's exactly that simple."

I stopped there. He moved his head stiffly, trying to ease his throat evidently. "Don' make me ask you theengs," he whispered. "Who sen' you there?"

My strap watch ticked away the seconds loud enough for me to hear it tick. I heard Lola North stir in her chair and the rain tugging at the windows and the clink of ice cubes in the blonde's highball.

I thought of the man across the desk from me, of his reputation in the days when liquor trucks rolled through Chicago streets with police escorts to beat off highjackers, of bodies turned into dust because Louis Antuni had wanted them that way. I thought of the man named Riley who was reasonably young and possibly pleasanter than he looked, of his companion who was old and silent and who did nothing but point a gun.

And all the while I was thinking these things Louis Antuni waited for me to make up my mind.

I said, "I was sent there by His Grace, Bishop McManus of the Catholic Church. Walsh called on him three days ago. When Walsh failed to keep a second appointment the Bishop sent me around to learn the reason."

He sat there like a boulder on a hill and looked six inches into my frontal lobes. And then he said the last thing in the world I expected to hear.

"I weesh to apologize to you, Meester Pine. When I read een the paper that eet ees you who fin' Vito, I theenk some wrong theengs. I theenk maybe you fin' some-theeng there besides Vito, that maybe you take thees theeng. I sen' a man to your office to learn eef eet ees there. He does not fin' eet."

"All he found," I said, "was a man's head. So he had to go and bounce a lead pipe off it. It was my head, Mr. Antuni."

He went right on, as if I hadn't spoken at all. "Later, I call up some people I know. They know you, sure. Tough guy, they say, but honest. All right. Maybe they don' know about Baijan, though—that maybe you work for heem. So I sen' for you to fin' out.

"You say you work for Hees Grace. All right. I know about heem. I already have a boy across the street there to see eef Wirtz he'sa go back."

I had to think back quickly before I could be sure. Then I was sure. I had called the man on Erie Street "Walsh" all the way through this conversation. I had been careful to do that. I remembered, too, the big fellow with the Palm Beach suit and the toothpick I'd seen across the street from the rectory. A vast wonder began to fill me. What had been a complicated matter to begin with was now a labyrinth of complications.

Antuni moved his hands restlessly along the desk's edge. He turned his head stiffly from side to side a time or two, trying to ease whatever was clawing inside his throat. Suddenly he began to cough, a harsh tearing sound like canvas being ripped. His hands tightened around the chair arms until his knuckles stood out white as sugar lumps. Tears squeezed from under the closed lids of his eyes as jagged pain twisted his face into a mask of agony the color of old snow.

By the time the spasm passed, Antuni's cheeks were dripping with perspiration and the lines around his mouth seemed deep enough to draw blood. He clawed a handkerchief from a pocket of his robe and mopped his face and neck. When he spoke again the words seemed wounded things barely able to crawl from between his lips.

"Dreenks, Callie."

The blonde climbed off the couch and moved her hips over to the liquor cabinet. She made the journey seem like a long, wearying trip across miles of monotonous prairie. Even drawing open one of the walnut panels was a job of work for her. She managed to turn her head without using both hands to do it, looked back over a flawless shoulder at Lola North and me and raised a thin high-curved eyebrow an eighth of an inch.

I wet my lips in anticipation. "Scotch and plain water," I said. I might even have been drooling a little. "Miss North?"

"Nothing, thank you."

It was a faraway voice, clear enough but without any

inflection to the words. I looked at her. Up to now I had been too occupied elsewhere to pay her much attention. She was sitting as relaxed as an old maid at a burlesque show. Her eyes were opened very wide and were fixed on a corner of Antuni's desk. They gave the impression of having been that way for a long time. To the casual glance she probably looked all right, but underneath she was inches away from hysteria. The touch of a hand would have sent her running up the nearest wall.

I didn't understand it at all. Being brought here at the point of a gun to face Louie Antuni's brown glare might have done that to her, but all that was past us now. The atmosphere of distrust and chill menace we had first walked into had been dissipated when I brought Bishop McManus' name into the conversation.

Antuni finished tucking away his handkerchief. "You steel hun' for Wirtz?" he mumbled.

"If you mean Walsh—yes."

"Name eesa Wirtz, Meester Pine."

"That may help me."

"For Hees Grace, hah?"

"That's it."

"How much he'sa pay you?"

"What everyone who hired me pays. Thirty a day. And too few at the price."

"How you like feefty gran', Meester Pine?"

"I'd have to keep my conscience to enjoy it."

A corner of his upper lip twitched. It might have been a smile. I never did find out. "An hones' man. I like hones' men, Meester Pine. Now an' then I meet one, but always far apart."

There was nothing in that for me to talk about. I would have liked to light a cigarette but I thought the smoke would probably bother him.

Very slowly Antuni said, "Fin' Wirtz for me, Meester Pine. First."

In the brief silence following his words I heard Lola

North catch her breath with sudden sharpness and the sound surprised me into looking at her. All her attention was still on that same corner of Antuni's desk, but the small white hands resting on the arms of her chair were balled into tight fists. Interesting as a reaction and possibly worth discussing—at an opportune moment. This didn't seem to be it.

To Mr. Big I said, "Why do you want him found, Mr. Antuni? You think he put that knife in your man?"

While I waited for an answer, the blonde swayed over and put a sweating glass in my hand. From her expression she might as well have been putting it on a table. The liquid in it was exactly the right shade of amber and there were two of the coldest ice cubes in the world bathing there.

I tilted the glass and took three long satisfying gulps. When I brought the glass down again my inner self was up off the canvas and flexing a bicep. The blonde was back at the cabinet and bringing out a chrome ice bucket holding a bottle swathed in a towel.

She undulated over to the desk, placed the works in front of Antuni and removed the towel, bringing to light a quart of champagne. The label was gaudy in the way French champagne labels are, and this was a brand I had never heard of. She drew the cork like an expert, getting a solid popping sound, filled a crystal goblet and put it where Mr. Big could reach it without straining. Then she went back to the couch and forgot us.

Antuni lifted the glass, twirling the stem slowly between the bones of thumb and forefinger while eying the contents without pleasure. Then very quickly he drank half while his free hand dug once more into the chair arm. He could wear out a lot of chairs the way he treated them.

He put the glass down with a small thump and massaged his throat with fingers that shook perceptibly. "Eesa no good for me. Makes the heart burn all night sometimes."

I said, "Then why drink the stuff?" It seemed the logical question.

His expression said I was an idiot. "Wha'sa matter weeth you, hah? Don' you know Louie Antuni dreenks only the best? I guess you don' remember the old days, hah?"

That let me see under the disease-ridden shell for the first time tonight. Here was an old man, a dying man, passed by and forgotten but still with enough money to supply himself with wine that disagreed with him and women he couldn't use. Yet he was still the Big Guy to himself and the boys he could hire; still the cop buyer and the jury briber; still the man who could order out the heavy artillery when the need arose.

Something of what I was thinking must have shown on my face. A trace of color flickered in his sunken cheeks and a shadow of his earlier anger burned in his brown eyes.

"Sure," he said, and the bitterness was unmistakable now, "Old Louie he'sa almos' finish. The doc he'sa say, 'Brain tumor, Louie. Maybe tonight, maybe eet'sa nex' year sometime.' All right. Sometheeng een my throat, too. The doc don't talk about thees, but Louie he'sa know. Hell weeth eet. Ever'body he'sa die sometime, hah?"

It was a long speech for him and it wore him out. I drank some more of my highball and glanced sidelong at Lola North while I waited. The radiator hissed away in its corner and the rain sounded far away. I tried looking at the blonde but she was beginning to wear on me and I gave it up. My head still ached, but nothing like it had ached two hours before.

The watch on my wrist pointed out that eight o'clock was still ten minutes away. I could hardly believe it. Tonight was to have been a quiet night: a bed and a book and a bottle next to a bucket of ice. Poor old Pine. The simple pleasures were seldom for him.

Antuni drank the rest of the wine in his glass. It took

another minute for him to recover from it, then he leaned wearily back in his chair, folded his arms once more across his chest and began to talk.

"You wan' to know why I say fin' Wirtz for me. Okay. Now I tell you a story, Meester Pine. Two, three months ago some pieces of paper she'sa come into thees country. A man and a woman breeng them from old country. These papers she'sa very valuable—more so than you can theenk."

He stopped there and breathed a while, resting his voice. I knew, of course, what the papers were, but he was supplying details I knew nothing about.

"The woman left thees man when they get to California. I don' know what happen to her; maybe he'sa keel her; ees no matter. But other people know about these papers an' wan' them very much."

He stopped again, this time to tilt the bottle with an unsteady hand and fill his glass. He made no move to drink any of it, however, but wet his lips with his tongue instead and went on with the story.

"Now comes a man name of Jafar Baijan. Thees Baijan ees very strange man, Meester Pine. Nobody he'sa know heem, nobody he'sa see heem, only few people know *about* heem. He'sa beeg-shot crook, Meester Pine, an' such a smart man. Only a job now an' then. Maybe years apart. An' only the beegest jobs he pull."

"What the books would call an international criminal," I said. "A behind-the-scenes guy who could get away with the Crown jewels if he put his mind to it and thought they were worth the bother. The pulp-paper magazines wore that one out years ago."

He sneered a healthy sneer. "Thees ees very funny to you, hah? Old Louie he'sa soft een hees head, hah? Jus' wait. You don' meet Jafar Baijan yet, Meester Pine, but you weel. Pretty soon I tell you why you weel."

He sipped a little of the champagne, not enough this time to hurt him much. He said, "Anyhow, thees man who breeng papers to thees country wan' to sell them. He'sa go to expert on old papers to get them like— like . . ." He groped for the word he wanted. "Like pedigree they the real theeng. You understan' thees, Meester Pine?"

"To get them authenticated," I said.

"Yes. The papers she'sa left weeth thees expert. An' that same night the man who breeng these papers to thees country, he'sa tortured and then beat to death in hees apartment. Jafar Baijan do thees to heem, Meester Pine."

He waited for me to say something. I sat there and swished the liquid in my glass and looked knowing and interested and said nothing. The blonde on the couch appeared to be sleeping.

"Okay," Antuni said. "Expert ees man named Wirtz. I don' ever talk to heem, so I don' know for sure what goes on een hees head. But I theenk eet would go like thees:

"Wirtz he'sa fin' out man who geeves heem papers he'sa been keeled. Wirtz he'sa look over these papers and he'sa know what they are. Okay, now he sell these papers, be reech, no one know about heem. So he'sa get een hees car and come to Chi to sell papers to Beeshop. Okay?"

"Okay," I said.

"Only—" he dragged out the word—"Wirtz he'sa forget one theeng: man that geeve heem papers he'sa tortured *before* he'sa keeled. He'sa tortured; that means who deed eet he'sa want to know sometheeng. He'sa keeled; that means he'sa talk first. Okay?"

"Clear," I said, "like glass. Okay."

"Fine. So the keeler—thees Jafar Baijan—he'sa know Wirtz have these papers. He follow heem to Chi to get them. But by thees time I know about these papers too. I wan' them very much. So I try to get them. First."

I said, "How did you learn about the papers and the story behind them?"

Antuni nodded and sipped at his glass. "Thees you
don' have to know. Louie steel have many friends, Meester Pine. Man who first have papers offer to sell them
to a man een California who ees friend of mine."

"Okay," I said. "I don't know how this friend of
yours knew the papers finally got into Wirtz's hands.
But you could probably explain that too—if it mattered.
Thing is, you found out Wirtz had been to see the Bishop
while His Grace was out of town. That told you who
Wirtz was trying to do business with. What I don't understand is why you didn't nail him when he went back
there three days ago."

Antuni shrugged hugely. "He'sa don' have papers
when he'sa go there then. Thees I know because papers
too beeg to carry aroun' een pocket. Would need beeg
envelope or briefcase. I wait until he go back weeth such
theeng. Only he'sa never go back. An' we lose heem."

"How did that happen?"

He flushed a little under his old-snow color. "Vito
he'sa watch rooming house. While Wirtz ees on way to
see Beeshop, Vito maybe go to hees room to look for
papers. Maybe Wirtz he'sa come back too soon an' keel
heem there. Or maybe Baijan who do eet. Ees no matter.
Either way, Wirtz ees afraid. He'sa know somebody after
these papers. So he run away.

By this time his old sick throat could hardly get words
through it. More to give him a rest than anything else,
I got up and went over to the cabinet to put together a
fresh drink. It would have been a shame to wake up the
blonde over such a small matter.

I returned to my chair, crossed my ankles and leaned
back, waiting for Antuni to give me the rest of it. Lola
North was a little less stiff in the face, a little nearer to
leaning back now. But not a great deal. Her eyes had
moved some, too—away from the desk and up to the
lamp standard on it.

A minute or two and Louie Antuni was ready to talk

again. He pushed his glass aside and leaned his forearms on the desk top while his eyes went over the collection of planes and hollows that make up my face.

"These papers," he mumbled. "Now I tell you about them, hah? Maybe eet'sa soun' crazy when I tell you. All right. I don' theenk eet'sa crazy, an' I don't care what you theenk. Okay?"

"Okay," I said.

"These papers she'sa very old. Two thousan' years old. Thees alone ees very strange, hah?"

"Not because of their age," I said, just to be contrary. "There are Egyptian papyri floating around three times that old."

"Hah!" That took care of Egypt and her scribes and my erudition. "Thees ees nothing to what I tell you now."

He took a deep, unsteady breath, and the flames were suddenly back in his eyes. "Meester Pine, the writeeng on these papers she'sa put there by Jesus Christ!"

Very quickly he made the sign of the cross with two shaking fingers, then sank back in his chair and closed his eyes.

Those last few words seemed to ring in the sharp silence settling slowly over the room. The blonde dozed on. Thunder grumbled outside as though from another planet. Seconds were born in pain and travail and grew into minutes and were thrown on the dust heap of Eternity. I fought to keep down a yawn.

The brown eyes across from me opened slowly. The flames in them were gone now, leaving two gutted cinders in skeletal sockets. Twice the thin unsteady lips parted and closed again as the ravaged throat strained to form words.

And when finally the words did come, they were sorry shreds of sound, audible but no more than that.

"Meester Pine, I have done bad theengs een my life. I don't have to tell you thees; ever'body he'sa know

about Louie Antuni. Pretty soon Louie, he'sa dead. But
first I wan' to make my peace weeth God an' the Church.
When I die I wan' a Requiem Mass an' to be put in
consecrated groun'. You understan' thees, Meester Pine?''

Out of an ocean of awe, I nodded.

He coughed a little, not much, nothing like before,
and got out his handkerchief and patted it against his
forehead.

He said, ''I weesh to geeve these words of Our Saviour
to the Church. Thees ees very beeg theeng for the Church,
you understan'. You help me to do thees, Meester Pine.
You help me to do thees one good very beeg theeng and
maybe the bad theengs Louie Antuni he'sa do weel not
matter too much.''

I said, ''As far as I know, Raymond Wirtz has the
manuscript. Bishop McManus has hired me to find Wirtz
for him. Presumably he doesn't want Wirtz without the
manuscript, although I'm sure he would take the manuscript without Wirtz. If that's clear.

''I'd suggest I bring Wirtz to you, provided I can find
him. You, in turn, buy the thing from him, if you can
meet his price. Then together you and I would go to the
Bishop and make delivery. I include myself, Mr. Antuni,
because the Bishop is my original client in this and he's
entitled to all the service I can give him.''

He nodded somberly. ''Like I say before, Meester
Pine, you are hones' man. We do thees like you say—
and when papers she'sa een Beeshop's han's, I geeve
you feefty gran'.''

''It sounds like a lot of money,'' I said.

He might not have heard me. He rubbed the handkerchief lightly between his palms, frowning. ''One theeng
more I mus' talk about, Meester Pine. Jafar Baijan. I
have learn many theengs about heem, an' yet I know
notheeng. He ees very smart—more smart than you and
me together. He ees keeler—he'sa keel anybody een hees
way. You don' meet heem yet, but I theenk you weel,

all right. Your name she'sa in newspaper about being in Wirtz's room. So you weel meet heem . . . an' he weel try to keel you, I theenk.''

"What does this mastermind look like?"

He shrugged hugely. "I don' know thees. Nobody knows thees I am told. Maybe Baijan he'sa not even a man. Maybe he'sa woman. Maybe he'sa Callie, here, who'sa make the dreenk for you. No, Meester Pine, I don' know thees.''

"It certainly leaves the field wide-open," I said. "It's possible that Baijan has already found Wirtz and has the manuscript. That would explain why Wirtz is missing."

He seemed to be having trouble keeping his eyes open and his head off his chest. He was old and tired and suffering, and his story was told. So much talking had emptied all the limited strength out of him.

He brought up his hand with an effort and pressed something under the edge of his desk. The door opened almost at once and Riley was standing there.

"Yeah, Louie?"

"My friend Meester Pine he'sa leaving. An' hees friend. Take them where you fin' them and be sure notheeng she'sa happen they don' like. You understan' thees, Riley?''

"Yeah, Louie.''

I put my glass down after emptying it, got the coats off the couch and helped Miss North into hers. She seemed in some sort of trance. After I scooped my hat off the floor, I said, "We came in my car. I can get along without an escort, but thanks just the same, Mr. Antuni.''

He nodded, his head barely moving, his eyes almost closed. "Eef sometheeng she'sa come up, you call me, hah? Number she'sa Kedzie 7324.''

He added a word that might have been Italian for good-by and held out a hand that was as light and fragile as four straws from a whisk broom.

I shook it gently, said, "Thanks for the drink," to the

blonde on the couch, got a blank look in return, and steered Lola North by the elbow toward Riley at the door.

On the way through, I glanced back over my shoulder. Mr. Big was still sitting the way I had left him. His eyes were closed all the way now, his head tilted forward and his lips moving in and out under shallow breathing.

The air on the porch was almost cold after the time I had spent in that hothouse of a room. Rain pattered through the sycamore leaves and gurgled along the eaves and bounced in puddles on the walk.

Riley leaned negligently against one of the pillars and lighted a cigarette, his nose seeming even more crooked in the match's brief flare, while Miss North and I were buttoning buttons and turning up collars. He said, "See, shamus. It wasn't too bad, hunh?"

"It's been a long day," I said, "and I've listened to too many people talk about too many things I don't understand. Good night to you. Ready, Miss North?"

"Yes." A small word, spoken by a small voice.

We left Riley standing there breathing smoke through a crooked smile and went quickly along the curving walk to where the Plymouth huddled at the curb. I helped her into the front seat and went around and slid in behind the wheel.

I looked back as we drove away. The heavy shadows of the porch hid everything but the bright end of Riley's cigarette.

# · 7 ·

"You didn't waste a lot of time moving out of the Stevens," I said. "You must have thrown your stuff in a suitcase, leaving a brassiere strap hanging out like they do in the funny papers, had them send a bellhop up with the bill, then slid out the back way."

She didn't say anything.

"You know all my secrets now," I went on. "If I had had any idea at all what that old man back there was going to throw in my lap, I'd have let them take you out the way he wanted."

She didn't say anything again. I looked at her briefly from the corners of my eyes. She was over about as near the car door as she could get, slumped there as if somebody had dropped her from a great height. In the faint light from the dash I could see her mouth hanging open slightly as though she lacked enough strength to keep her lips together. Her eyes were closed and her golden head bobbed with the car motion. Alone and helpless, worried and afraid. Needing a strong masculine arm about her waist and a shoulder in a rough tweed jacket impregnated with the smell of pipe tobacco to put her head against.

I swerved around a Ford coupe driven by an elderly party who had read too many safety posters about the dangers of driving on wet pavements. Thunder prowled the sky, using lightning flashes to find its way. Slow anger began to rise in me—vague and impotent and without meaning.

I set my teeth and said gently, "I'll have to know, Miss North. You can understand why, can't you?"

She stirred slightly and the hands lying loosely in her lap twisted tightly together, came up slowly about half-way, then fell limply back. It was a gesture of despair, almost theatrical in its intensity. But no words, no change in the slack lines of her face. I took a deep breath and got ready to make another try. . . .

"I can't tell you." A quiet voice, clear enough, but with panic seething under its surface.

I watched the road ahead, the raindrops bouncing in the silver path of my headlights, my hands tight on the wheel. "Why not?" I said.

"You're against him, too. You and that evil old man and the police. I won't tell you a thing!" Her voice began to rise. "None of you! Not ever!"

There was a side street directly ahead. I spun the wheel into it and braked to a halt fifteen or twenty feet from the intersection, letting the motor die. I turned toward her then, seeing the white, startled oval of her face and the dark depths of eyes that were now wide-open and filled with alarm.

I said, "I'm glad you feel up to discussing this, Miss North, and I'd rather not divide my attention by driving at the same time. Will you have a cigarette?"

"Please."

I got them out, lighted hers and one for myself, and pushed the vent open a crack for air. She turned to face me, bringing her knees up on the seat for comfort, giving me a long and defiant glance while exhaling a white fan of smoke.

I said, "First things first, Miss North. This 'him' everybody's supposed to be against is Raymond Wirtz. Is that right?"

Silence as defiant as her eyes.

"What's he to you, Miss North?"

The line of her jaw hardened and she shook her head. Not a word. Not ever, she had said.

I sighed. "The last time we met you pulled my fangs for me and walked out. Not this time. You tell it to me, all of it, or down to the Homicide Bureau you go and right into the lap of a sergeant named Tinney. I'm not fooling, Miss North."

This time I got a curled lip thrown in my face. It peeled away the helpless child veneer and made her the competent, self-possessed young woman I had run up against on Erie Street. But I got a few words too.

"You wouldn't dare turn me over to the police. I'd tell them about everything: what that manuscript really is and about Antuni and the Bishop. Once those things came out you'd never get what you're after."

She had me there, although not for the reason she seemed to think. Bishop McManus was my client and his interests wouldn't be protected by having this story spread in headlines.

I sat there and dragged on my cigarette and let her wallow in a pool of triumph. When I figured she was about as self-satisfied as she could get, I let her have the other barrel—the loaded one.

"You're so right, Miss North. You've heard some things tonight that mustn't get out. So we'll keep away from the police. Instead we're going back to Antuni's place. I'll tell him where I ran into you this morning and I'll tell him about this little talk. Then I'll leave you to him and walk out."

For a second, there, I thought she was going to topple over in a dead faint. The cigarette rolled out of her fingers to the floor boards, terror poured into her face and she swayed on the seat. I put out a hand to steady her and the touch of my fingers against her arm seemed to close a circuit. The next thing I knew she had her head against my chest and her fingers digging into my arms and she was crying: great long tearing sobs that shook us both.

I let her go to it while I snaked out one foot and set it down on the ember of her cigarette. I blew the soft strands of gold away from my nose and mouth and breathed in the subtle odors left by her last shampoo. I listened to the rain and the whisper of tires from the cross street behind us and the sounds of a girl crying out her heart. I wondered what kind of reception private detectives got from St. Peter.

Finally she sat up and tried wiping her eyes with her fingers, ending up by taking the handkerchief out of my breast pocket to finish the job. She blew her nose delicately into it and sniffled a time or two and pushed her hair out of her eyes. I felt like a man who spends his days kicking kittens off the sidewalk.

"That was silly of me," she whispered. "I'm sorry about your handkerchief. I came away in such a hurry I forgot my bag."

"Think nothing of it."

She blew her nose again, not so delicately this time, and asked for another cigarette. I held a match for her, saw that beyond needing a touch of face powder, which I couldn't furnish, she was pretty much her old self again.

She stared straight into my eyes over the match flame. "You wouldn't do that, Mr. Pine? What you said?"

I waved out the match and dropped it into the dashboard tray. "I'm hoping you won't force my hand. But a man hired me to do a job, Miss North, and I intend doing that job, if it's at all possible."

"Even if it hurts an innocent person?"

"You've got to convince me that innocence has something to do with it."

She rested an elbow against the seat back and dragged deeply on her cigarette. Words came out behind the smoke—words that tumbled over each other in their rush to get out.

"I need help, Mr. Pine. Desperately. I don't know which way to turn. I'm in a strange city and I don't have a great deal of money. I know you're working for somebody else, but by helping me you'll be helping him too."

The flow of words stopped abruptly and she turned

her head away from me. When I was sure that was all I was going to get, I said, "What's your interest in Raymond Wirtz, Miss North?"

Her head came around quickly. "Then you'll help me?"

"How do I know whether I'll help you? I've got to know who I'm supposed to be helping and why. Let's wind this up, for Chrisakes. I've been hit over the head and pointed at with a gun and buried in words. Right now I want to know one thing: *What's your interest in Raymond Wirtz?*"

". . . He's my husband."

I breathed in and out. "Un-hunh. All right. That lifts the fog a little. Go on from there."

It took her a long time to assemble the next sentence. "It's a not uncommon story, Mr. Pine. I thought I was in love with him."

"But you're not now?"

"No. I—don't think so."

"Which is it: no or maybe?"

She sighed. "I'm all mixed up inside. I met Raymond two years ago, Mr. Pine, at the university. He was very much like my father—as well as I can remember my father. Charming, intelligent, handsome and with a wonderful sense of humor. And yet like a child in many ways: absentminded and helpless . . . it's hard to put into words. A month after I met him we were married. It lasted less than a year. He . . . was too old for me."

She bent forward and put a cylinder of ash into the tray, straightened again and made a vague movement with one slender hand. "It's all rather pathetic, and I'm afraid it doesn't put me in a very nice light. But I'm young and human. . . ."

Her words trailed off and a long moment dragged by before she spoke again. Then: "I used to see him occasionally—afterward. He aged a lot in that year, and there was a bitterness in him that had never been there

before—a cynical attitude where once had been that gentle,
wonderful sense of humor. Each time we met he'd ask
the same question: when was I going to divorce him and
get myself a rich husband?''

"Why a question like that?"

Her eyes were on something beyond the car, beyond
the street, back into two years that belonged to the past.
"That's the horrible part, Mr. Pine. He thought my reason for leaving him was because there was so little money.
Raymond's earnings, both as a faculty member and a
paleographer—even a world-famous paleographer—were
small. I couldn't tell him the real reason I was leaving
him; I couldn't be that cruel. And so I blamed it onto
his inability to give me the material things I wanted, or
claimed I wanted. As if money would have made that
much difference!"

"But in spite of all this," I said, "you come running
to Chicago after him."

She turned her head to give me a long level stare. "In
one way or another," she said tightly, "I feel it's largely
my fault that my husband's in trouble. I'm trying to make
amends by getting him out of it. That's why I followed
him to Chicago."

I pushed what was left of my cigarette through the air
vent and stretched as much of my frame as the limited
space would allow. "Go ahead," I said wearily, "and
tell me. Pour out the words. My spirits are low and my
ears are numb, but I'll listen. Other people read books
or go to the fights or walk in the sun or make love. But
not poor old Pine. He just sits and listens."

She said stiffly, "This was your idea. You wanted to
know these things."

"Yeah. Go ahead and tell them to me."

Her fingers gave a sudden convulsive jerk to the handkerchief she was holding. My handkerchief. She drew
in on her cigarette and blew out a cloud of smoke that
hung writhing in the air between us until a damp breeze

from outside tore it apart. By the time all that was over with she was through seething and able to trust her voice.

"He called me three weeks ago, while we were both in Los Angeles. He was so excited and incoherent I could barely understand him. He said he had got hold of something that was worth millions of dollars, that it was his alone and that he was leaving for Chicago immediately to sell it."

I said, "Why tell you about it?"

"He was getting even with me for leaving him, gloating over what he called my 'mistake.' Frankly I thought he'd brooded himself into a nervous breakdown and might do something desperate. The minute he hung up I hurried over there but he was already gone. One of the neighbors said he'd seen Raymond load suitcases into his car and drive away not more than an hour before."

I took off my hat and rubbed the tender spot on the back of my head and listened to the rain while I thought about Raymond Wirtz as this girl had sketched him for me. A gentle, scholarly man who had spent his years digging among musty papers, until one day he ran headlong into sex and had it bash his character and personality out of shape. Not a nice picture but one that, with variations, has been painted too many times.

I said, "Let's see if I can guess the rest of it. Out of the depths of compassion and a feeling of guilt you came on to Chicago to iron out the kinks in your husband's battered ego. Is that it?"

That stiffened her spine, and while the lack of light hid the anger in her eyes it was there just the same. "I can't say I care for the way you've expressed it, Mr. Pine." Very cool, very controlled, very phony.

"Is that important? How did you locate him here?"

Her sigh said that I was impossible but that she would forgive me. "I telephoned a private detective agency in Chicago and hired it to pick up his trail when he drove into town. I was notified where he was staying, then I came on to join him. You walked in on me while I was in his room.''

"You certainly carry compassion to great lengths," I said. "It's a lovely story, Mrs. Wirtz, but I'd like it even better if you would include a few words about how all his talk about millions of dollars had something to do with your decision to come out here."

"Is that what you think of me?"

"Yes. Did I do wrong?"

She watched me out of a face filled with shadows. "You may be right, Mr. Pine. Actually I didn't spend a great deal of time weighing motives. But the fact remains that Raymond's in serious trouble, both because of the body found in his room and because there are persons who want that manuscript badly enough to kill him for it."

"That's right," I said. "What do you want me to do about it?"

"I want you to find him—for me. I want you to help me get him out of Illinois and back where he belongs. I want his life spared, Mr. Pine, for if anything happens to him, I'll always blame myself!"

"And what about the twenty-five million dollars?"

She gasped. "Twenty-fi——"

"Yeah. That's the price he quoted the Bishop."

"Good heavens, I didn't realize it amounted to anything like *that!* Let's worry about that after we find him. I want him to be s-safe."

"There's still this business of a corpse being found in his room. The boys down at Homicide will want that straightened out."

She shivered slightly and rubbed her arms with unsteady fingers. "I—know. But they're looking for a man named Raymond Walsh whom nobody knows anything about. If Raymond can get out of the state, they'll never discover his true identity. Unless you tell them."

. I got out another cigarette, lighted it and started the car motor. I said, "I work for my clients and my conscience, Mrs. Wirtz. I co-operate with the police but I don't do their laundry or haul their garbage. But there are three other people who know Wirtz and Walsh are the same man: Louie Antuni, Bishop McManus and a man named Myles Benbrook, a friend of your husband. If I find Wirtz I am not going to turn him in. But if you're as intelligent as you seem you'll sell him on surrendering voluntarily to the police. If he put Post out of the way it was most likely self-defense—if your husband is the kind of man you tell me he is.

"But all this is jumping the gun. First, he's got to be found—alive."

While she was chewing that over, I shifted gears, turned the car around and drove the few feet back to the boulevard, turning east there.

After four or five blocks, she came out of a silence to say, "Are you going to help me find Raymond, Mr. Pine?"

"Two people have already hired me to find him, both for the same reason. You might as well be number three, particularly since you're his wife. I'll keep you informed—within reason. Where can I drop you off?"

She told me, naming a fairly expensive apartment hotel near the lake front and well out on the North Side, adding that she had no idea how long she would have to remain in town and an apartment would be a lot more convenient and no more costly than a good hotel room. It seemed a lot of information for such a small question.

Twice during the ride back she tried to make conversation, but my response was too brief to be misunderstood, and the last couple of miles held nothing but silence.

At Estes Avenue east of Sheridan Road stood a gray monolith with the words LAKE TOWERS in neon on its roof. I pulled into the curb in front of the entrance and reached past her to open the car door. "Good night, Mrs. Wirtz. It's been quite an evening."

She started to slip out, stopped and looked back at

me. What I could see of her face told me nothing of what was going on behind it. "Good night, Mr. Pine. It certainly has."

She bent suddenly, kissed me full on the mouth, whispered, "Good night, Paul," and was gone in a rustle of cloth and the flash of nylons, running lightly across the walk and through one of the two revolving doors.

I drove on east another fifty feet until I found a driveway, used it to turn around in the narrow street and pulled in next to the curb at a point where I could watch the Lake Towers' entrance.

I waited twenty minutes but she never came out again. It appeared Lola North had been truthful about one thing, at least.

# · 8 ·

I was working as an elevator operator in a coal mine—anthracite probably—and the cage was down about four thousand feet with its controls stuck. Up on the surface some guy was leaning a heavy thumb against the bell button, filling the shaft with a high keening sound. . . .

I woke up in the middle of swinging one hand. It hit against the telephone on the nightstand next to me and knocked the receiver out of its cradle. That stopped the bells, but as far as light was concerned I was still in a coal mine.

I sat up, my mouth filled with unspoken curses, and bent my wrist up until I could see the illuminated dial of my strap watch. 1:12. In the morning. I bent sideways over the edge of the bed and fumbled around, found the dangling receiver and got it into position against my ear.

I said, "Yeah. What d'ya want?" Even to my ears it sounded as cordial as a lion at feeding time.

"Mr. Pine? I was so afraid you weren't in. This is Mr. Pine, isn't it?"

A voice I almost didn't recognize. A voice trying to be calm and even a little stately, and not succeeding worth a darn. The voice of Bishop McManus and probably as excited as a bishop's is permitted to get.

"This is Pine, Your Grace. Awake, now, and reasonably clearheaded."

"He just called me Mr. Pine. Just this minute. He wants to turn the manuscript over to me, but he's af——"

"Hold on a minute," I said. "I want to turn on a light."

I sat there in the darkness with the receiver glued to my ear and listened to a high windy silence along the wire. It was the wrong kind of silence and that told me what I had wanted to know. I said, "I'm going to say something, Your Grace. Don't hang up until I explain what it means."

It puzzled him but he was game. "Very well."

Very loudly I said into the mouthpiece, "Get off the wire, you snooping son of a bitch, before I come down there and pull you off!"

The gasp came from His Grace and the faint click from a switchboard key being closed. Then the high windy silence was gone, leaving only silence.

Into that I said, "The language turned out a little stronger than I intended, but we have a night clerk here with more nose than an anteater. You say Wirtz called you?"

"Yes." He seemed to have his excitement fairly well controlled now. "He wants to place the manuscript in my hands, Mr. Pine, then leave town. But he's afraid to come to the rectory. He's quite worked up, nearly hysterical with fear. Claims the police are closing in on him because of that body found in his room. He even has an idea the rectory is being watched."

I remembered the big man in the Palm Beach suit, his toothpick and his newspaper. Louie Antuni's man. I said, "I think he's right. And it's not only the buttons who are after him."

"What do you mean, Mr. Pine?"

"It's a long story, most of it fantastic. What does Wirtz suggest?"

"He wanted me to meet him on a street corner out in the northwest section of Chicago. Obviously it is impossible for me to do a thing like that at this time of morning. I'm not able to drive a car, for one thing, and

I wouldn't care to take a taxi. I suggested he send it to me by messenger, but he refused. Said there was only one person in Chicago he could trust and that he was beginning to have doubts about him. The man was almost incoherent, Mr. Pine.''

"There's probably a good reason behind his incoherence," I said. "What arrangement did you finally make. Assuming of course, that you made one.''

He hesitated for a few seconds, then came out with it—in a rush of words.

"I'm afraid I've taken a great deal for granted, Mr. Pine. You see, I told him that while I wouldn't be able to come there myself, I would send someone whom I trust implicitly.''

He paused to give me a chance to get set for a shock. But the shock had come and gone by this time. I was way ahead of him.

I said, "It'll be a pleasure to wind this one up, Your Grace. I was afraid it wasn't going to work out this easy—if it does. Where do I meet him and when?''

He sounded as happy as a pup with a new bone. "At the southwest corner of Sacramento Boulevard and Glenlake. At two-thirty. About an hour from now.''

I repeated the instructions, then said, "He won't quibble over giving it up, will he?''

"Oh, no. Just say to him, 'Good morning, Mr. Smith. Do you have a book for me to read?' ''

It gave me my first laugh in the past twelve hours. "Sounds like a day in a rental library. Whose idea was that?''

He laughed a little too. "Mine, I'm afraid. He wants to be sure you're representing me.''

"Fair enough." I yawned, covering the mouthpiece first. "I'll be there on time, Your Grace.''

"I'm really very grateful for this, Mr. Pine." His voice was solemn now. "Call me, please, at Wabash 9900 at your first opportunity after you have the manuscript. After that I'd like you to come directly to the rectory. I'll arrange to let you in myself."

I remembered the arrangement with Louie Antuni. A call to him at the same time I called the Bishop would give the old man a chance to meet me in front of the rectory.

I nodded before I realized a nod was wasted, and said, "I'll be able to call you between, say, two-forty-five and three."

"I'll be right here," he said simply.

He broke the connection and I snapped on the night-stand lamp before replacing the receiver. I pushed back the light blanket and put my feet on the floor and stared at them without interest. They looked large and white and slightly obscene, the way bare feet do in the morning. I yawned again and pawed my hair and scratched my sides through my pajama top. The bottle of Scotch stood stiff and tall beside the lamp, but the bucket for ice cubes had only water in it now.

I lighted a cigarette from the pack next to the Scotch and wavered into the bathroom to splash water on my face and comb my hair. I wondered why I bothered. A face leered back at me out of the mirror—a face I hardly knew and instantly disliked. Its tired eyes were bloodshot and the skin around them had been left six months under a stone. The face of a private detective, without a future and without hope.

In the kitchen, I put fire under a pot of coffee and went back to the bedroom to dress. Dark trousers that needed pressing, good enough for the rain I could hear against the window; a soft-collar shirt and the first tie my fingers came across. The shoes needed a shine but this wasn't my night to go dancing.

Two cups of the coffee, hot as the bowels of Vesuvius and touched up with a few drops of black molasses rum, made a new, if not better, man of me. I put the cup and saucer in the sink, got my suit coat and trench coat out of the closet and laid them on the bed while I strapped on an underarm holster and put my one gun—a .38 Colt Detective Special—into it.

In case I met Fu Manchu or Dillinger. Or an unknown quantity named Jafar Baijan.

I pulled my hatbrim down over my eyes, went out and rode the elevator to the first floor. A pool of light marked the desk, with Sam Wilson, the night man, behind it at the switchboard, his hands and eyes filled with a pulp-paper magazine. I could see the picture on the cover from across the distance. It would have given nightmares to Jack the Ripper.

Wilson jerked up his head before I reached the counter. He stood up quickly and came over to the opposite side, reflected light glinting on the thick lenses masking his muddy eyes. His sagging lips were trying to smile but not with much success. He was worried and I knew why.

I said, "I'm saying this once and only once. The next time you leave the key open on me you'll have to climb a flagpole to wash your ears—if you ever do. Is that clear?"

His thin voice shot up to a screech like an E string. "Aw gee, Mr. Pine, you got me all wrong. Honest, I don't listen in on your calls, Mr. Pine. I wouldn't dream——"

"That's all," I said. "Don't wait up for me."

I was three steps on my way to the front door when he said wistfully, "Another big case, hunh, Mr. Pine?"

I stopped to turn around and look at him. I had hurt his feelings but not enough to dent his curiosity. You couldn't have dented it with a cold chisel. His round sagging face brooded at me, patches of hair where the razor had skidded standing out in the bright light.

"Just to keep you in touch," I said, "I'm on my way to pick up twenty-five million bucks."

He shook his head sadly and turned back to the switchboard. I pushed open one of the heavy doors and went out, standing in the recess while buttoning my collar around my neck.

It was still raining, not so heavy as before but still enough of it not to go out in if you had your choice. I ducked south along the walk, dodging what puddles I could, and on into the Plymouth.

The motor started with understandable reluctance. I lighted a cigarette I didn't want and rolled south along Wayne Avenue between twin rows of parked cars. An occasional lighted window in the buildings along there marked where people were still up and playing bridge or raiding the icebox or arguing over the family budget. Not Pine, brother; he was out hunting a case of pneumonia.

I turned off at Pratt Boulevard and on over to Western. It was getting to be a familiar route.

Glenlake Avenue came in a stone's throw south of Devon and Sacramento was six blocks west of Western. The district was still in the subdivision stage: a good many empty weed-covered lots interspaced with bright new houses surrounded by freshly seeded lawns that were black and gooey mud under the rain. The homes themselves were a long way from being pretentious, but they had that nice solid middle-class look that went with the folks who lived in them.

I drove slowly past the corner where Wirtz was to be waiting with a fabulous manuscript under his arm and his heart in his mouth. He might have been there but I couldn't see him. There were too many trees and far too little light for me to see anything. My wrist watch put the time at two-thirty-three.

I went on by and another block south. More trees, more empty lots, more houses. It didn't seem anyone was tailing me with a long black car filled with machine guns. I made a complete turn at the end of the block, my headlights picking out the words on a realtor's tin sign nailed to a stake.

Three-quarters of the way back to the proper corner I drew up at the curb, got out into the wet, jaywalked to the south side of Sacramento and on down toward Glenlake. No sounds except the drip of water and my shoe soles slapping concrete. A bleary street lamp picked up my shadow and threw it away out ahead of me.

At the corner, I cupped my hands around a match flame and lighted a cigarette while I peered south and west along the walks. Nothing moved along them but more shadows and more rain. No man with a manuscript and only one man without one. Me. I felt as conspicuous as the Swedish minister to Liberia.

I blew smoke through my nose, coughed lightly and walked around in a tight circle. The strips of parkway were lined with large trees so close together their upper branches intermingled. Around their boles was no light at all. Ten men could have been hidden within twenty feet of me. I hoped there weren't. Maybe Wirtz was standing behind one of those trees, watching me.

He had watched me long enough. Out loud I said, ''Hey, Mr. Smith.'' The words sounded plaintive and not very robust, muffled by the weather. I decided not to try that again.

I took the gun out and held it along my leg and set out to prowl the parkway strip west along Glenlake. And at the base of the fourth tree down I found him. I found him a split second before I stepped on his head.

He was stretched out, face down on the wet grass and beyond caring about it. In the darkness he was just a long lumpy shape with a bent elbow sticking out and the hand below it underneath him somewhere. A small dim object near his head was a snap-brim hat and a sequin of light from the distant street lamp touched the design on one of his socks.

It wasn't necessary to hold a mirror to his lips or hunt around for his pulse. His pulse would be missing and his soul gone to wherever souls go after the motor stops.

You can always tell, even in a bad light, when they lay limp as wetwash in the tub.

I bent down part way and said, "Good evening, Mr. Smith. Do you have a book for me to read?" Then I laughed, hollowly, briefly and without humor, and knelt beside the body and struck a match. With my free hand I lifted the head by its hair and looked at the face. . . .

It was the face of Sergeant Frank Tinney.

It was four in the morning, still dark, still raining, still miserable. I was sitting in a low-backed armchair in a cubbyhole of an office at the Summerdale station. I had been sitting there, alone, for over ten minutes now, and getting fed up with it.

The door opened and closed, and the same lieutenant from Central Homicide who had listened to my story four times already during the past hour, sat down behind the desk and across from me.

He was a lean, soft-spoken man a year or two past fifty, with neatly combed black hair graying at the temples, sharp steady eyes and a chill manner. At least what I'd seen of his manner was chill. A plain maroon bow tie nested high on his white shirt and his lightweight brown suit was just off the rack. His name was Overmire, and tonight, over a fresh corpse, was the first time we had met.

He moved some papers aimlessly about on the ragged green desk blotter. They were papers that had something to do with zoning violation complaints and had nothing to do with me. I knew that because ten minutes is too long just to stare at walls and your fingernails.

He pushed them aside finally and sighed the deepest sigh in the world. Without looking at me, he said, "I talked to the Bishop, Pine. His story bears you out."

"I gave you the truth, Lieutenant. That's why it bears out."

He sighed again and put one of his stubby-fingered

hands palm down in front of him. His face seemed a little grayer and his lips even tighter than an hour before. He said heavily, "Tinney was a good man. A wife and two kids—the youngest just three. She's going to miss her dad."

I didn't say anything. Smoke from my cigarette moved sluggishly in the room's stale air.

Overmire leaned back in his chair and rubbed the back of one hand slowly against the top of his thigh. "Let's go over it once more, Pine. In case you forgot something the first three times."

"Four," I said.

"All right, four. You're lucky it's not going to be forty. We get on the touchy side when one of our boys gets pushed."

I said, "Yesterday morning, around ten-thirty, I called on Bishop McManus. At his request. He told me a man named Raymond Walsh had called on him three days before and tried to sell him a rare and valuable manuscript. Walsh was to have returned the next day with the manuscript. He failed to show up. The Bishop asked me to go out to the address Walsh had given and see why. I did and I found a body in the closet of Walsh's room. I notified Homicide and Sergeant Tinney came out. I told him what I've just told you.

"At one-seventeen this morning Bishop McManus telephoned me and said Walsh wanted to meet him, the Bishop, at the corner of Glenlake and Sacramento. At two-thirty this morning. The Bishop said he couldn't keep the date himself but he would send me. I went out there at the right time. I didn't find Walsh, but I did find the body of Sergeant Tinney. I immediately drove to the Granville el station and called Homicide from a phone booth there."

The lieutenant put his right hand around his right kneecap and squeezed it until his knuckles showed. "A cop killer," he muttered. "The son of a bitch. The lousy son

of a bitch." He let loose of his knee and reached for the
papers again and pushed them another two inches toward
the telephone. His voice got up to normal again. "Nothing else, Pine?"

"Not a thing."

"I wouldn't want to find out different later on."

"Yeah."

He slapped his hand smartly against the blotter, so
suddenly it made me jump. "We'll get him," he growled.
"As sure as Christ we'll get him. We know a lot about
him already, Pine. Tinney really worked on this thing.
We know he's from Los Angeles, we know his real name
is Raymond Wirtz, we know his background. A goddam
university professor. How d'ya like *that?* When those
boys go sour they really go sour. All of that came out
of leads from the clothing and stuff found in his closet
out on Erie Street."

He struck the desk top three light measured blows with
the bottom of a fist. "All that we found in Tinney's
reports. But nothing at all in them to tell us how he
happened to know Wirtz was going to be at the corner
of Glenlake and Sacramento this morning. But he did
know it and Wirtz was there and Wirtz killed him. Killed
him the way he killed Willie Post: a long-bladed knife
and smack-dab into the heart."

He called Wirtz what he had called him twice before
and sighed again. "We've covered every hotel and rooming house in this town. Tinney was doing that in a small
way; now we're doing it in a big way. Maybe that'll
uncover Wirtz. We've got the best description the Bishop
could furnish. It could fit a thousand men but we've got
it. Los Angeles is mailing us a photo if they can find
one. We'll get him, Pine, and when we do he'll fall
down a lot of stairs before he goes to trial."

I didn't say anything. He leaned halfway across the
desk and put his crossed forearms on the blotter and
impaled me with those chill eyes. "I'm a reasonable

man, Pine. I have a lot of respect for most of you private guys and recognize the help the Department gets from them occasionally. While it never got out to the public, your part in the Sandmark case* is in the records and I've read them.''

He stopped there and looked off into the distance and thought his thoughts. I scraped a thumbnail against the stubble on my chin and just sat.

"All right," he said suddenly. "You can go. You can go because of what I know about you and because you're working for Bishop McManus . . . maybe *only* because you're working for him. Your story fits with his and that's good enough for me. Up to right now, anyway. But the next time—if there *is* a next time—Wirtz tries to make a date with either of you, I want to know about it. In advance, mister.''

I stood up and swung my hat against my leg. "Good morning, Lieutenant."

He nodded briefly. I put on my hat and went out the door.

*Halo in Blood, 1946, The Bobbs-Merrill Company.

# · 9 ·

Nine-thirty was early for me to be at the office any morning. But I had wakened about eight o'clock, dull-eyed and unhappy and filled with a vast restlessness that had no answer.

It was a dreary, rain-swept day, raining the kind of rain that comes out of a sky the color and texture of a flophouse bed sheet and goes on and on. I opened the inner-office window behind its glass ventilator, put my hat and trench coat on the customer's chair and poked my shoe toe at the windrows of office junk left on the floor by yesterday's prowler. The cleaning woman must have taken one look at the wreckage and gone downstairs to quit.

I pushed most of the stuff back into the desk drawers and the rest into the wastebasket. By the time I was through I was ready to go back to bed. I yawned and sat down in the swivel chair and spun the telephone dial a few times without lifting the receiver. For practice. I tried thinking about the Bishop and Wirtz and a few sheets of papyrus, or whatever, worth twenty-five million dollars. Nothing came of it. I tried thinking about Louie Antuni and Lola North, or Lola Wirtz as it had turned out.

Nothing came of that, either.

And right then, in the middle of lighting a cigarette, I remembered something I never should have forgotten.

I dug out the classified directory and started checking

off public garages in the vicinity of the seventeen-hundred block on West Erie Street. After half an hour's work I figured the list was long enough.

The nearest was on Huron Street just west of Ashland. I dialed the number shown and got hold of a deep-south accent against a background of motor noises.

I said, "Is Wirtz's car still on the floor?"

"Who dat?"

"Wirtz," I said. "Raymond Wirtz. A Chevvy coupe."

"Ah cain't rightly heah you, mistuh. Gimme dat name agin."

"Wirtz!" I yelled. "W-i-r-t-z. Like in liverwirtz. You got his Chevvy coupe out there?"

"Hol' on a minute, mistuh." The receiver went down, leaving me with the motor noises.

I leaned back to wait and to ogle the red-haired girl on my Varga calendar above the filing cabinets. It was a calendar with a fresh page and a different pose for each month. This being May, she wore a green play suit about half the size of a microbe's necktie. She was weaving a daisy chain, but her green eyes hinted she could think of better things to do with her time.

"We-all don' sto' no cah fo' nobody lak that, mistuh."

Another half hour and five more calls added up to the same answer. Maybe it hadn't been such a hot idea, after all. But number six paid off big—a public garage out on West Superior, near Damen. The man who answered the phone owned the place and evidently it was small enough for him to know all his customers by name.

"The Wirtz Chevrolet?" he said. "Sure, it's here. Hasn't been out, to my knowledge, in the last three, four days."

"Anybody been checking on it?"

"Only you, mister. What's the angle?"

"It may be a bender," I said. "Report from the West Coast says it was picked off a Los Angeles street about three weeks ago."

He stuttered over that but finally admitted the job was wearing California pads. I remembered hearing somewhere that car owners out there usually carried their registration certificates strapped to the steering post. He checked up when I mentioned this, but came back and said there was no sign of one. He called me "officer" at the time. It was his idea—I hadn't said I was from the Stolen Auto Section—and I didn't correct him.

"Okay," I said. "There'll be a man out sometime today. If Wirtz calls for it before then, tell him the battery's dead, or something. Might be a good idea to work a wire or two loose, just in case."

He said he'd do that and he hoped we wouldn't think he was running a hot car farm. I gave a noncommittal grunt, which proved to him that I was a Department man, and hung up.

I made a note of the address, picked up the receiver again and called Michael Light at his home. Mike did leg work for me now and then—a wild-eyed Irishman, smart, fast, tough, built like a light-heavy. He wore a wooden left arm to replace the one lost under wheels one zero night while on duty as a railroad dick. He and his wife lived on a pension, but he still liked to play cop and I was able to use him now and then.

When he came to the phone I explained about the car. "It's at the Cushman Garage, 1944 West Superior. Get out there and take a look at it. When you're sure you'll know it, when and if it pulls out, tell the guy in charge our tip was a bum one; that you've got nothing on this particular heap and to forget to mention it when the real owner comes around. If he wants credentials, flash one of those insurance cards you carry."

"I can handle it."

"Yeah. Then you park where you can keep an eye on the entrance. I want full-time service on this, Mike. Chances are the place closes nights; some of those outlying garages do. If not, arrange for a relief."

"And if somebody takes her out?"

"Then tie a string to it. Lose that buggy and I'll skin you for a banana."

"Any time I louse up a job, brother, I loan you my skinning knife."

I put back the receiver. I had a lead now, a nice warm one, and I basked in its heat for a minute or two. I had used a brain cell. A little late, but not too late.

More time went by while I sat there and fouled the air with smoke and scratched the back of my neck and dangled my foot. Rain, in soft small drops now, tapped lightly against the window and dripped a lonely rhythm on the brick ledge outside. Cool, clean-smelling air came in over the ventilator top and rattled the cords on the drawn Venetian blind. A gray and misty day. A day for an easy chair and a book and a bottle of brandy. A day for honeymooners, for sleep, for ducks.

The telephone rang.

When I answered, a voice, female and familiar, said, "Is this Mr. Pine, the private detective?"

"Confidential investigator sounds so much nicer," I said. "And how's His Grace behaving this morning?"

It earned me a small gasp. "You recognized my voice!" She sounded pleased for some obscure reason of her own. "Why, he's still sitting up there in his office, Mr. Pine. Just *won't* stir out of it and won't even talk to anyone on the telephone. He even has his meals sent in. He's waiting for someone or something special and I've had to turn everyone away. I'm really worried about him, Mr. Pine; he's bound to have a nervous breakdown or impair his health if this strain he's under doesn't end real soon. If he'd only just come down and visit with me like he used to. He sleeps in the bedroom next to his office and has the only night line connected to his phone when I close the board for the night."

I should never have asked such a leading question. I said, "Does he want to talk to me or was this your own idea?"

"Oh, *no!* I mean it wasn't *my* idea at all. He asked

me to. I wouldn't *dare* take it on myself to—to snoop into his affairs. Although I do wish there was something . . .''

She paused, to catch her breath probably, and I jumped into the opening. "Put him on. I'll try to cheer him up for you."

"Oh, I do hope you can! If he would only———"

I cleared my throat right in the middle of her sentence, and she understood what it meant. "I'm sorry, Mr. Pine." She closed the key and rang His Grace's phone.

"Yes?" Rich and sonorous on the surface; underneath, a sort of impersonal eagerness if that's possible.

"This is Pine, Bishop McManus."

His breath rustled along the wire. "I was afraid you might not be down this early, Mr. Pine. I decided against ringing your apartment, in case you were still sleeping."

I had a vivid picture of what the last three days had been to him. Sitting there surrounded by redwood walls and leatherbound books behind glass, with his hand never very far away from the telephone in case it should ring and announce that Raymond Wirtz was downstairs to keep the long overdue appointment. Or perhaps pacing the floor with measured tread, hands clasped behind his back, his mind torn between the belief Wirtz had started a hoax too big to finish and the wild hope he was on the verge of the Christian era's greatest discovery.

"I could have used it," I said, "but I'll have to put it off for a while."

He didn't speak again for a few seconds. Then he said, "I was afraid the police might be holding you. I was very careful to assure Lieutenant Overmire that you were acting solely on my behalf and that I would appreciate any effort to keep our names out of the newspapers. It was thoughtful of you to call me this morning in advance of notifying the police."

"I was being selfish," I said, "and I'm loose right now because of you. It's something new for me to have a client who's really influential."

He brushed that one off. "I suppose now we're right back where we started," he said wistfully. "This is getting to be quite a problem, isn't it? I can't very well transact business with a murderer . . . but then we don't know beyond doubt that he is a murderer, do we?"

I grinned at that one. It was a pleasure to learn that bishops were as human as the next guy. Here he was, clinging to the last shred of doubt of Wirtz's guilt in an effort to assure himself that dealing with the man for the manuscript was ethical.

I said, "I can report some progress, Your Grace. I've managed to locate Wirtz's car in a public garage near the Erie Street address. Now that the heat's on him for fair because of this cop killing, he may try to get out of town in it. Then, too, I'm seeing a woman, a Mrs. Benbrook, whose husband is an old friend of Wirtz's. He disappeared the same day Wirtz was seeing you and I think the coincidence is strong enough to mean something. I may be wrong—it could be woman trouble instead. I hope to find out for sure this afternoon."

His voice perked up noticeably. "Excellent! I have every faith in you, Mr. Pine. Please keep me informed on any new developments."

I said I would and that ended the conversation. In one respect, at least, the Bishop was turning out like almost every other client: he wanted satisfaction and he wanted it with the speed of light. In his case, however, there was the best reason in the world for wanting it that way.

More time passed while I sat there woolgathering— and an inferior grade of wool at that. The mailman came and pushed a telephone bill and an advertisement through the inner-door letter drop and went away.

I ate an early lunch for want of something better to do, and spent a few hours browsing in a department-store book section. I picked up a new mystery by William P. McGivern and took it back to the office to read.

At two in the afternoon I marked my page and put the book in the same drawer I formerly kept my bourbon in, took my hat off the filing cabinet and went out into the rain to earn my living.

The Myles Benbrooks lived along the best section of Sheridan Road, two blocks south of Devon, in one of those eighteen-room rock piles the idle rich call homes. It was at the southwest corner of an intersection, set back in the middle of a huge lot that was mostly flower beds and dark green lawn behind a seven-foot hedge.

A pair of elderly white elms drooped spreading branches over the cross street side of the property, and a big southern cottonwood held lacy gray-green curtains in front of the upstairs windows facing the Lake.

I swung the Plymouth left into the cross street and up to the curb a short distance above the entrance to a crushed stone driveway that made a wide bend behind lilac bushes and disappeared at the rear of the house.

I got out into the rain and locked the car, although it seemed hardly necessary in this neighborhood, and went quickly along a glazed concrete walk and up three steps to a sprawling rough-stone porch with a flat roof, black-and-red-mosaic tile flooring and a low railing loaded with flower boxes painted a dull green. Several green and yellow canvas chairs stood here and there, also an enormous swing suspended by chains, its padding covered in yellow waterproof chintz.

A yellow reed table held an overflowing ashtray, three empty highball glasses and last week's copy of *The Saturday Evening Post*. It seemed the wrong kind of weather for porch lounging. Probably left over from yesterday.

The doorway was wide enough to bring in the groceries without leaving the truck and was barred by a hunk of polished teakwood and leaded glass too heavy for its hinges. I found a bell button set among some brass scrollwork and gave it the stiff finger.

If anything rang anywhere I didn't hear it. I took off my hat and shook away some of the water, put the hat

back on and wiped my hands dry with a handkerchief.
The only sounds were the rain in the gutters around the
porch top and the motor growl of a new dark-blue Buick
convertible turning the corner, water splashing from under its wheels.

I was reaching for the bell button a second time when
the door swung silently back and a tall thin character in
gray cuffless trousers and a black alpaca coat looked at
me from a face that was mostly nose and teeth.

"Good afternoon, sir." A soft voice, polite, correct,
colorless as air.

I made it brief for him. "Paul Pine. To see Mrs.
Benbrook. I'm expected."

"Certainly, sir. This way, if you please."

I followed him into a wide cool-looking hall paneled
in blond mahogany and with a graceful sweep of carpeted
stairs far back in the dim distance. He took my hat and
trench coat and hung them away in a closet, and we went
down the hall, our feet soundless against yards of carpeting as rich as butter and as old as Methuselah's grand-
father, around a corner and more miles along another
hall with a vaulted ceiling this time and a row of French
doors at the far end overlooking the grounds.

Halfway down, the butler opened a door, announced
my name and stood aside to let me through.

It was a pleasant room, not too large, furnished to
point up an old-fashioned fireplace with a log fire crack-
ling behind a heavy copper screen. A red-leather chesterfield, seduction-sized, faced the fire across a very
large, very white, wool throw rug. On the mirrored top
of a heavy walnut coffee table were highball glasses, a
siphon bottle, copper pitcher and ice bucket, and a fifth
of the kind of Scotch that is seldom encountered but
never forgotten. Over near the three windows was a baby
grand piano with sheet music on the rack and a fringed
gold scarf hanging almost to the floor.

She was sitting in a wingback chair near the fireplace,

a book in her lap, a tall glass in her hand and a small smile on her very red lips. She was dressed to stay home and drink liquor, wearing a sea-green something too frilly to be a dress and not frilly enough to be a negligee. There were pearls at her throat and one at the lobe of each ear.

Her nice throbbing voice said, "Nice to see you again, Mr. Pine. Do sit down and make yourself a drink. I decided Scotch would suit you. Was I right?"

"Indubitably," I said, to prove I was a college man and worthy of sitting in her drawing room. I found a place on the chesterfield across from her and put Scotch in a glass with plain water from the pitcher on top of that.

I tested the mixture and damn near emptied the glass before I remembered this was liquor I was drinking. She was watching me with approval. Evidently drinking men were right down her alley.

She said, "I took the liberty of inquiring about you, Mr. Pine. I hope you don't mind."

"How did I make out?"

"Very well. My husband's attorneys spoke glowingly of you."

"Good for them." I tried my drink again, being a little more gentlemanly about it this time. "Did they want to know why you were asking?"

"Oh, no. Mr. Scott was curious, of course, but he didn't come right out with it. How does your head feel this afternoon?"

"Round as ever, thank you. Does he know your husband is missing?"

"Not yet. I thought I'd wait a few days. Too much of a fuss might be embarrassing if Myles should show up with some perfectly reasonable explanation."

She put her head back and tied into her drink with the easy grace of a practiced drinker. The book slid off her lap to the floor and she ignored it. It had been nothing but a stage prop anyway. Connie Benbrook wasn't the type to curl up with anything as inanimate as a novel.

The rain made cheerful sounds beyond the windows and the fire made popping noises behind its screen. I got out my cigarettes and offered her one and lighted them both with a silver table lighter shaped like a small gravy boat. She gave me a melting smile by way of thanks and I went back to the chesterfield and refilled my glass. She finished her drink quickly while I was doing that and I made her another.

When we were comfortable again, I said, "Back to business. No word from your husband at all?"

"No."

"The mystery woman hasn't called back, the one you listened in on the day he disappeared?"

"No. Why should she? He's probably with her right now."

"Raymond Wirtz hasn't been around looking for him?"

"No. Nothing has changed since I saw you yesterday afternoon."

"All right. I had to be sure, is all." I took a long drink and shook my head a little getting over it. "Do you have that list of people who might be hearing from him?"

She blew out a long ribbon of smoke and tilted her glass again before answering me. "I'm afraid not," she said carelessly. "Outside of his bank and perhaps his lawyers, I wouldn't know who to put down."

"You do want him found?"

That one got me stared at. "Certainly. Why would I have engaged your services otherwise?"

"Why, indeed." I emptied my glass and reached for the bottle again. "Maybe we should look over your husband's address book and personal papers. For a clue. I need a clue, Mrs. Benbrook. A bright shiny one with a little arrow painted on it and words saying, 'He went thataway.'"

She laughed softly and finished her glass, her throat muscles rippling as she swallowed. Before I could get up to take the empty glass and fill it for her, she was out of the chair and tilting the Scotch bottle. She put in a jolt to stagger a Kentucky mountaineer, waved the water pitcher in its general vicinity, and took three smooth rustling steps around the coffee table and dropped down beside me on the couch.

Her brown eyes seemed to lick their lips. "You're awfully good-looking," she said deep down in her throat. We drank to that.

I said, "You're as lovely as a jungle night." We drank to that.

I wondered if a jungle night was really lovely, then decided it would be if there were panther eyes to reflect the moon. Three highballs had done that to me.

The glasses were empty again and I filled them, remembering just in time that *some* water should be used. She leaned close—very close. Under its thin covering of sea-green silk her arm sent out warmth that soaked through my coat sleeve. She smelled like an orchid looks. I bit into my glass to keep from biting into her.

She said huskily, "What do you do on long rainy nights?"

"I'd hate to tell you."

"A scrapbook, I bet. Pasting in clippings on the cases you've solved."

"They wouldn't fill a matchbook folder."

We drank to my lack of clippings. I said, "We'll never find him, this way."

"Do you need two hands to hold one glass?"

I transferred my glass to the other hand and put my free arm around her. A smooth supple waist. My fingers tingled. She leaned against me and breathed deeply. Not half as deeply as I was breathing. I turned my head the necessary half-inch and kissed her. I kissed her hard enough and long enough to make it count.

We had a drink.

I said, "About your husband . . ."

"Can't it wait?" Her voice was a panther's purr, her breath hot against my cheek. "It's Paul, isn't it?"

"Uh-hunh."

"Kiss me, Paul."

I kissed her. Her mouth came to pieces under mine and her hand slid up and inside my shirt. I let my free hand move around experimentally. Nothing interfered; all the signals were set in its favor.

We had a drink—and the glasses were empty. My hand floated over and picked up the bottle. Dry as the oasis in a mirage. I shook it. Still empty.

She was leaning back, her eyes closed, her mouth slack with desire. Her hair was mussed and smeared lipstick made her mouth misshapen. We were a fine pair. I said, "Party's over."

The long lashes swept up to reveal a blank stare. "What'd you say, Paul?"

I showed her the bottle. "All gone," I said. "Somebody went and drank it."

"The bell cord's next to the fireplace."

I went over to it. I hit my knee against a corner of the coffee table on the way over. The door was opened by a small white-haired man in a dark coat and striped trousers. The footman, I judged. I had the sketchy education in such matters that the movies furnished. I pointed at the empty bottle and he bowed four inches from the waist and said, "At once, sir," and went away. I wondered what he thought of us. About what the French populace must have thought of Marie Antoinette.

By the time I was back to the couch the footman was in again—this time with a copper tray holding two bottles, more ice cubes and another pitcher of water. He shifted them to the table, cleaned up the debris and left, closing the door like slamming a cloud.

I made two drinks and handed her one and sat down again, this time two feet away. I said, "It's a beautiful afternoon and I'm enjoying every minute of it. Now let's talk about finding your husband."

She was smart enough and experienced enough to keep her true feelings under cover—except for her eyes. They said I was less than one-tenth a man and a damned fool besides. She had every reason to think it, right then.

"Finding Myles is up to you," she said coolly. "I'll tell you what I can, of course."

I said, "I have a strong idea about your husband, Mrs. Benbrook. I think he's around town some place, helping Raymond Wirtz take care of a matter."

She wasn't particularly interested. She drank some of her drink, her hand as steady as Gibraltar on a calm day. Strong drink would never mock her.

"What sort of matter?"

"A matter of money. Lots and lots of money. Enough money to kill people over."

"Are you saying Myles has killed someone? That's ridiculous."

I put down my glass and lighted cigarettes for us both. The Scotch was stirring pleasantly under my belt. It was the kind of Scotch that would die easy in you.

I said, "A man died last night, Mrs. Benbrook. This morning, really, about two-thirty. He was a policeman who was hunting Raymond Wirtz."

"Raymond isn't the type to kill people."

"Is your husband?"

That careful, still look I had noticed the afternoon before veiled her eyes. "I think this is getting out of hand, Mr. Pine. I want you to find my husband, not accuse him of murder."

I grinned at her. "A minute ago you were calling me Paul."

"Damn you," she said. And then she laughed. "I'm not through with you yet, mister!"

"What about Myles? Is he as broad-minded as he is rich?"

She shrugged and she wasn't laughing any more. "The hell with him," she said recklessly. "I need young men— men with the sap of life in their veins and a good strong back. Myles is too old for me."

I said, "Another woman said almost the same thing to me last night. What's the matter with you dames? You make a guy afraid of reaching his forties."

She retreated behind her glass. I sipped my drink and puffed on my cigarette and listened to the fire.

I said, "Back to this dead policeman, Mrs. Benbrook. His fellow officers are upset by his murder. They're going to find Wirtz, but soon. When they do, it'll be too bad for him."

"If he's murdered someone," she said indifferently, "anything that happens to him will be deserved, won't it?"

"It goes a little deeper than that. The cops will do some swinging on whoever's been hiding him out. I may be wrong but I think that's where your husband comes in."

She stiffened slightly, and away back behind those lovely brown eyes thoughts were being born—thoughts that went just so far because they needed more to feed on. I was the guy to feed them.

"You think Myles is hiding Raymond Wirtz from the police? Why would he do that? I mean, Raymond and he weren't such close friends that he would leave himself open to a charge of accessory to murder."

"I don't think friendship has anything to do with it, at least from your husband's standpoint. I think he's doing it for gain."

"Why, that's impossible !" A good ripe round sneer went along with that statement. "Myles has more money than he could use in a dozen lifetimes, and Raymond Wirtz is practically a pauper. You're being absurd, Paul."

I said, "Raymond Wirtz came to Chicago with an article worth millions of dollars. And I mean millions. He came here to sell it to the one market that could pay his price. He had a comparable market in Los Angeles, but he had got hold of this article in a kind of unlawful way and was afraid to peddle it so close to home.

"When he reached Chicago, he found the man he expected to deal with was out of town. Wirtz was worried at the delay. He needed a friend to confide in, someone who was wealthy enough not to have designs on this valuable possession. Your husband fitted that description and Wirtz came to him and told his story. He may have borrowed money from him to tide him over the two weeks or so he had to wait.

"When the time came, Wirtz went to call on his market. A deal was made and Wirtz returned to his room. To his horror he found a dead man in his closet. That sent him into a blind panic. He knew then someone else, someone who thought nothing of human life, was after what he had. He ran to your husband, Mrs. Benbrook."

I paused to dampen the dust in my throat with Scotch. Constance Benbrook wasn't indifferent any longer. She was hanging on every word, and the more I said, the more she was beginning to see what I had thought she would see.

"Your husband decided to help Raymond Wirtz foil his enemies. I say enemies because there were two of them now—the one who had killed Willie Post and, in a body, the police. I think he was satisfied Wirtz himself hadn't pushed Post, so in his own mind, at least, he wasn't shielding a killer. But I do think the real reason he was willing to go to such lengths to help Wirtz was because he wanted this valuable article for himself."

I waited while she fixed herself another drink. I still had better than half of my last one. She drank a quarter of it and sank back and nodded. "Go ahead. This is very interesting. I'm not so sure it's true."

"Early this morning," I said, "Wirtz telephoned this man he hoped to make a sale to, asking him to meet him at an out-of-the-way spot to make delivery. This man refused but suggested the article be delivered by messenger. And right there Wirtz said a very significant thing."

I stopped again and took a pull at my glass. Connie Benbrook sighed. "All right. Enjoy yourself. What did Raymond say?"

"He said there was only one man in Chicago he could trust and that he was beginning to doubt him."

"You think he meant my husband?"

"The evidence points that way, doesn't it?"

She shrugged. "What happened then?"

"I had already been hired to find Wirtz—which will explain to you how my name happened to be in the paper as the one who found Willie Post. This man called me and asked that I meet Wirtz and pick up the article in question. I kept the date, but instead of meeting Wirtz I met a body, the body of a man who had been hunting Wirtz for Post's murder. Being a cop he found him, while I was still chasing a long fly to center field. The cop got the business end of a knife for his brilliance. And that brings you up to date, Mrs. Benbrook."

"And your deductions, Mr. Holmes?"

"Simple. You have the same answer already. Either Wirtz killed the cop to keep from being tossed in pokey, or Myles Benbrook did it for him."

She stood up swiftly and put her glass down on the table. "I see that I've made a mistake," she said harshly. "In trying to find my husband I've thrown him into a murder case. I suppose you're going to the police with this?"

"You suppose wrong," I said. "I don't *know* who killed Post or this cop, and the police are interested only in facts. You're a client of mine, Mrs. Benbrook, and as such you're entitled to know the score. I've just given it to you. My job right now is to find your husband before the police do—if he's with Raymond Wirtz. I think he is. You're hiring me to find *him*—not what he's been up to."

"You mean you'd protect a murderer?"

"Not ever, Mrs. Benbrook. But I'm not going to try

to prove anyone's a murderer, either, not unless I'm hired to do it.''

She gnawed a lip and, still standing, picked up her glass and poured the stuff down her throat. It ended up with a lot of company. "I honestly haven't the slightest idea where Myles is."

"I believe that. Otherwise it would have been pointless to hire me to find him. But we'd better start digging for something that may lead to him."

"Let's go into the library."

I followed her out into the hall and back the way I had come, around the same corner and through one of a double set of doors.

It was a huge book-lined room, with brown leather chairs and divans and a Spanish refectory table as long as a bowling alley down the middle. The west wall was French windows that opened onto a narrow terrace. Gray light from the overcast sky did little to relieve the gloom of the dark wood walls.

Over near the windows was a small desk which must have come out of some eighteenth-century monastery. But its drawers were equipped with modern locks. Connie Benbrook removed a book from a near-by shelf, felt behind it and came up with a ring of keys.

Nothing that meant anything came out of the drawers—until we reached the last one. A brown metal document box was in there. I took it out for her and she found a key on the ring to unlock it. Filled to the brim with papers. Insurance policies, deeds, copies of legal-looking papers, a will consisting of twelve or fifteen pages of single-spaced typing. You need a lot of property to make a will that long.

So far neither of us had said a word since we entered the room. I snapped on the desk lamp, sat down in the leather chair behind the desk and began to sort through those papers. "I'd hoped to find an address book," I said while spreading them out.

"I don't know of one."

"Sit down and relax. This may take some time."

She lighted a cigarette and sat there smoking, watching my every move. I found a blank sheet of paper in one of the drawers and began copying down names and addresses shown on the instruments. The list stretched out longer and longer the further down the pile I went.

"I think you're wasting your time, Paul."

"Uh-hunh. That's the way police work goes, Mrs. Benbrook. A ton of sand for a grain of gold. I'll sit in my office and run up a telephone bill and probably end up with nothing but a sore ear. But I have to start somewhere."

The third paper from the bottom of the pile was the copy of a mortgage. A six-room house, brick, seven years old, valued when the mortgage was executed at $17,500, including the lot. Dated three years and two months before. Payments at $100 a month, for the full amount. That last made it a little unusual. There should have been some kind of down payment. Purchaser: a Mrs. Irene Taylor. Address of property: 6018 North Rockwell Street. Across the face of the copy was scrawled, *Paid in Full, Myles Benbrook*. Under that was the date of final payment—a date that showed the life of the mortgage to have been exactly seven months.

I sucked thoughtfully at a tooth. Connie Benbrook said, "What is it, Paul?"

"I don't know. Who is Mrs. Irene Taylor?"

She was silent long enough to surprise me into looking at her. She was staring at me, frowning. I said, "It means something to you, hunh?"

"She was Myles's secretary before he retired from the brokerage business."

Her voice sounded just odd enough to tell me more than her words. I said, "Like that, hunh?"

She flushed solidly behind what was left of her make-up. "I don't know for sure. And stop saying 'hunh' in that repulsive way!"

"Okay. What *do* you know, even if it isn't for sure?"

"Some of Myles's friends have wives who were thick with the first Mrs. Benbrook. They don't like me. To prove they don't like me, they've dropped a few hints about my husband and his former secretary—all in a helpful spirit, you understand."

"What do the hints add up to?"

"Exactly to what you're thinking." She threw cigarette ashes on the rug with a sharp movement of her hand. "When he married me that ended it. I'm positive of that. Let's see what you've got there."

I handed her the duplicate mortgage. She looked it over. By the time she was ready to give it back she knew as much as I knew but nothing at all of what I had guessed.

"So he gave her a house." She shrugged one shoulder. "All right. He could afford it. One way of pensioning her off, I suppose. Why should it interest you? Are you thinking he's deserted me for that cheap little divorcee?"

"No," I said. "Your husband isn't interested in women right now, Mrs. Benbrook. I'll check with her, though, just like all the rest on this list."

I wrote down the name and address below the others, just as I did the names and addresses from the remaining two documents left in the pile. Then I pushed the heap together, lined up the edges and replaced them all in the brown metal box. Mrs. Benbrook turned the key in the lock and I returned the box to its drawer.

We sat there a while in the silence and thought our thoughts. The cone of light from the desk lamp winked back from the diamonds in her wedding ring and brought out the color of her hair.

Finally I glanced at my strap watch. "Four o'clock, Mrs. Benbrook. Time I got back to my milk route."

She said softly, "I keep thinking of those two bottles on the coffee table."

I patted one of her hands and stood up. "Uh-hunh. But the ice is probably all melted by now. You can't drink the stuff without ice. Good-by and thanks. I'll keep you informed.''

She went with me to the library door and nodded coolly when I said good-by a second time. The butler, his expression as distant as the stratosphere, gave me my hat and raincoat and let me out into the rain.

The Plymouth's interior never looked shabbier and, after all the elegance I had just been exposed to, never more welcome. I looked at myself in the rear-view mirror and winced. No wonder the butler had held himself aloof. In his place I would have run for bandages and the iodine.

I scrubbed the stuff off with my handkerchief, ran a comb through my hair and drove away from there.

# · 10 ·

6018 North Rockwell was one house in a row of houses all apparently off the same drafting board. Red brick, green trimming at the windows and door, a cocky little wind vane on the gabled roof. The front and side lawns were neat and the grass seemed healthy. A small porch was set off center at the front, its shingled roof supported by two square concrete posts, with the house number in shiny black metal nailed to the one on the right.

I spent a couple of minutes giving the bell a workout with no result. A thin white curtain covered the glass in the door. Not thin enough, though, for me to see through. I rattled the knob, but this time there was a lock behind it. I wouldn't have gone in anyway.

I left the porch and followed a trim ribbon of cement around to the rear. The back porch was wood, painted the same green as the window trim and a lot more orderly than most back porches. Nobody answered my knock and what I could see of the kitchen revealed nothing more startling than the lack of dirty dishes in the sink. I discovered I was already thinking highly of Mrs. Irene Taylor.

I leaned against the bannister and looked out over the grassy back yard to one of those revolving clotheslines on a post and a rose arbor beyond that. Nobody around except the rain and me. I was beginning to feel on the depressed side. That would be Connie Benbrook's Scotch.

I went out to the Plymouth at the curb and crawled

slowly in behind the wheel. It had been a wasted effort, one more in a lifetime of wasted efforts. I wouldn't have made it at all except that a woman very close to Myles Benbrook was living there, plus the fact that 6018 North Rockwell was exactly three and a half blocks from where I'd found the body of Sergeant Frank Tinney.

At five o'clock I ate pot roast and the trimmings at the Ontra. I took a late edition of the *Daily News* back to the office with me, boosted the window a few inches, turned on the desk lamp and sat down to read Sydney Harris' column.

Three hours dragged by. Nobody came to see me, the phone didn't ring, and the only sounds were of traffic eight floors below. Rain still dripped endlessly with the aching dismalness of a Jewish funeral. There had been no mail on the floor under the chute, no telegrams came, nobody cared whether I lived or died or moved to Terre Haute.

By eight-fifteen I had all I could take. I had gone through everything in the paper except the want ads, there was a mound of cigarette butts in the ashtray, and my tongue tasted like something rejected by a scavenger. I glowered at my wrist watch, growled, "Up the creek, brother!" for no reason at all and put on my trench coat and hat.

The fat little dentist in the next office was locking his door for the day as I came out into the corridor. He nodded to me. "Good evening, Mr. Pine. You're later than usual."

"And all for nothing," I said. "I nearly came in to have you drill one of my teeth. Just for something to do."

His smile was a little sad in a dignified way. "I could have used the business, sir."

We rode down in the same uneasy elevator, out to the street and our separate ways. Lights from neon signs and shopwindows cast patterns in color on wet sidewalks and streets, while citizens hurried by with their heads bowed against the rain. The corner newsstand at Wabash Avenue had its back to what little wind there was and its sideboards up to protect the papers. Water dripped from the el platforms and there was a sodden rumble to the sound of trains overhead.

I picked up my car at the parking lot and took Dearborn Street to get out of the Loop, heading north. At Chicago Avenue I turned west to Damen, then south a block to Superior Street and on around the corner.

A narrow, deep, one-story red-brick building between two sagging frame houses on the north side of the street was the Cushman Garage. The dust-streaked office window held a display of spark plugs, and beyond that a fat man in shirt sleeves sat reading a newspaper under a shaded bulb hanging from the ceiling. The green folding doors at the car entrance were closed and one of the red lights flanking them was out.

Fifty feet further along, on the same side of the street, a battered Ford Tudor stood at the curb, nose pointed in my direction. I parked across from it and went over and opened the door on the sidewalk side.

The muscular guy behind the wheel was Michael Light. I said, "Haven't you anything better to do?" and slid in next to him and closed the door.

The rain bounced softly against the roof and ran in unsteady lines down the windshield. The air was close and reeked of oil, rubber and stale cigars. Light put out a large hand and took a cigarette from the pack I extended.

"Christ! Since twelve-thirty this morning!" His voice was harsh, tired, angry. "You know what I had for supper? A lousy ham sandwich and a thermos of coffee." His knobby face stood out in the match flare. "For ten bucks a day . . . and I don't even need the money."

"You get a look at Wirtz's car?"

"Certainly I got a look at it. You think I'd be roosting here if I didn't? There's been cars in and out of that joint all day long, and half of 'em Chevvys. This is a poor man's neighborhood, brother. You don't get no limousines here."

"Give me a picture of it."

"Forty-one club coupe, light gray. Right rear fender's got a dent about the size of a baseball where somebody put the end of a bumper. Orange and black California license, number 7F26-419."

"Uh-hunh." I turned out the no-draft panel to let in some air. "You got that number any place besides in your head?"

"Yeah." He fished a white business-size envelope out of his coat pocket and gave it to me. "I wrote it on that."

I put it away. "The guy in the garage tell you anything about Wirtz?"

"Not much you can use. When I told him I wanted a look at the car, he said he knew all along something was wrong about Wirtz. Said he acted like something was on his mind: kept looking over his shoulder and kind of sneaked around. You shoulda seen his puss when I tell him the Chevvy wasn't the car I wanted. It suddenly hit him, I guess, that he'd been running down a customer and the customer might find out about it."

"Find out if they stay open all night?"

"Only till one in the morning. Open again at six. What do you want me do?"

I thought about it for a moment. "Go on home, Mike. I can't think of a better way to spend a rainy night than to sit in the street and watch a rathole. Be here again at six. I may be able to give you a few hours' break during the afternoon. You got a gun on you?"

"Yeah. Such as it is. Iver-Johnson .38."

"Better let me have it. Just in case."

He leaned past me to the glove compartment and brought out the weapon, watching me as I slipped it into a side pocket of my trench coat. He said, "What goes with this Wirtz, anyway?"

"A client wants to talk to him."

"That's all?"

"Yep."

He laughed shortly. "Ten bucks a day and no answers. Okay, you're the boss man." He pinched out his cigarette with the black fingers of his artificial hand and switched on the ignition and the lights. "See you tomorrow."

I got out and he drove away. I went back to my own car, turned it about in the narrow street and cut off the motor. The radio gave me static and a beer commercial, but it wasn't my night to be fussy.

The hours moved by like ten-ton trucks pulled uphill by snails. Blackness and damp all around. There were other cars parked along both curbs behind me but none of them seemed to be occupied. Now and then the garage doors ground open to let in or discharge a car, but only two of those coming out were Chevrolets and neither a gray club coupe. The rain grew heavier around eleven and I pulled up to within twenty feet of the entrance for better visibility.

By midnight traffic was down almost to nothing. I watched the shirt-sleeved man put down his paper, drink a container of coffee and light a cigar before disappearing through an inner door. Getting ready to shut up shop. It seemed I had wasted a long evening.

At twelve-forty-five I threw away my cigarette and was reaching for the switch when a man on foot turned the corner at Damen Avenue and came briskly up to, and through, the office door of the garage. He was reasonably tall, certainly slender and wore a gray topcoat and hat, with the brim of the latter drawn down over his eyes.

It could have been Raymond Wirtz. It could have been any other tall slender man too . . . and it probably was. I started the motor turning over quietly, switched off the radio and kept my eyes on those folding doors.

They clashed open finally. Headlights cut twin pathways through the night and a light gray Chevrolet coupe rolled slowly into sight, along the short driveway, then swung west, away from where I was parked. I had a clear spot wiped on my windshield even while the garage doors were opening; through it I made out a rounded dent in the Chevvy's right rear fender.

It seemed Mr. Wirtz had called for his property.

I waited, with my headlights out, until the gray car was through bumping across the trolley tracks on Damen and a quarter block beyond that. Then I switched on my parking lights and took up the chase. All I wanted now was to learn where Wirtz was holed up. Afterward would be time enough to push in and ask questions.

During the first ten or twelve blocks he must have turned that many corners. Not that he knew he was being followed: he wanted only to learn if that was the case. He used only side streets, and it took all my experience to keep him in view and not be spotted myself.

And all the time these maneuvers were going on, we were getting farther and farther into the western part of town.

At Chicago Avenue and Kedzie, where the car line turns east for a few blocks, Wirtz evidently decided no one was interested in him. He turned north into Kedzie and sharply increased his speed.

This was a well-traveled street, fairly wide and mostly residential this far out, and there was a fair amount of traffic even at one-fifteen on a rainy morning. I cut down the space between us to half a block and stayed there by holding the needle on the forty mark. The Chevrolet stayed well out toward the center of the street, while I kept in nearer the right-hand curb to keep my lights out of his rear-view mirror.

The blocks spun by. Traffic signals were green for us most of the time, although twice we waited out red lights almost side by side. There were enough cars, however, to keep me from being conspicuous, and he never caught on.

Two or three blocks north of Belmont Avenue, the Chevrolet began to slow down at each intersection, the way a driver will do when he's trying to make out street markers at night. I dropped back until he was a full block ahead . . . and that's how he trapped me into showing my hand.

It happened at the intersection of Kedzie and Addison. There, the coupe came almost to a full stop, waited until a car passed in the opposite lane, then made a left turn into Addison. I was half a block behind at the time and I tromped on the gas, made the same turn . . . and met him coming back out.

I had a brief glimpse of a white, staring face through water-streaked glass . . . then he was past me and swinging north again on screeching tires into Kedzie. By the time I finished a complete circle and lit out after him, he was a block away and hitting fifty.

There was no longer any point in being cunning. I laid a heavy foot on the accelerator and went after him with blood in my eye. He probably knew he had a plaster by this time, but even if he didn't, he thought so. That was just as bad—for me.

His first mistake was trying to throw me off by turning practically every corner he came to. He cut them narrow and fast, the coupe teetering like a fat woman on a waxed floor. But I had much more experience at this sort of high jinks and the distance between us began to shrink fast. Then he made a stab at pulling away from me by shoving the gas pedal through the floorboards while keeping in a straight line. That was no good either, because there was more power under my hood and I was using it.

His big mistake, though, was in not heading back toward heavily traveled thoroughfares. He might well have lost me that way; at worst he could have kept me from doing any more than following him. But with all the turning and twisting, he might have lost his sense of direction. Only in a dim way did I know where we were myself.

The last street he picked to outrun me on had only a few houses to each block, with stretches of open ground between. Few street lamps and those far apart. No other cars around and no one on the sidewalks.

Gradually I began to inch up until I was almost abreast the coupe. I could see him bent across the wheel, head stiffly erect, driving like a dirt-track champion.

A corner loomed ahead. I saw one of his hands shift high on the steering wheel. I snatched my foot from the gas and set it lightly on the brake. Tires gave a banshee wail as the Chevrolet made the turn.

You don't make that kind of turn at that speed on wet pavement . . . not if you expect to go any farther in the same car. The coupe's rear end skidded wide, kept on skidding, slammed against and over the curbing and struck with a tangled crash of breaking glass and twisting metal into the trunk of a cottonwood drooping its branches across the parkway.

I was out of the Plymouth and over there while glass was still showering the asphalt. The rear right side was caved away in and the wheel there jutted out like the open lid on a can of beans. The gun Light had loaned me came into my hand while I was reaching out to jerk open the door.

He was slumped across the wheel, arms hanging down, the white blob of his face turned to me. In the weak rays from the intersection light I could see his eyes, open and staring at me.

I showed him the gun. "Out, Buster. With your hands where I can watch them."

"Who are you?" His voice shook. I could hardly understand the words.

I said, "I'm a guy with a gun. Do you come out under your own power or would you like to fall out on your face?"

He lifted his head slowly, shaking it to clear away the shock. He slid painfully across the seat ducked his head through the opening and stepped into the street. Out where there was better light. I could see a small trickle of blood seeping from the hairline above his left ear.

He wet his lips. "I—I insist on knowing who you are."

"Turn around," I said, "and keep those hands over your head."

When he tried protesting I gestured with the gun in a tough way and the words died in his throat. I patted him in the proper places and found nothing more deadly than a ball-point pen.

I stepped back and said, "Okay, Wirtz. Where's that manuscript?"

"Wh-what?" He wheeled sharply to face me, frenzy twisting what I could see of his face. "I don't know what you're talking about. Who are you?"

I got out my deputy sheriff's star and let him have a glimpse of it. The light wasn't strong enough for him to identify it as anything more than a star. But that was good enough for him.

"The police!" His sigh of relief almost shook the gun I was holding. "I thought you were somebody else. A— a holdup man."

"You mean Jafar Baijan, Mr. Wirtz?"

It was a shot in the dark, and like most shots in the dark it didn't hit anything. He wouldn't have known the name of the man responsible for the torture and death of the man who first brought that manuscript into this country.

His expression told me that. Before he could speak, I said, "I know everything, Mr. Wirtz. I could start a quiz show with what I know. The manuscript, what it is and where you hoped to sell it. I know about the Bishop and the twenty-five-million-dollar asking price and about your wife being in Chicago hunting for you.''

He put a hand up slowly to touch the blood on his cheek as if first aware something foreign was there. He looked at his fingers with a kind of vague horror, took a handkerchief from his breast pocket and mopped away the blood. He said hazily, "I think I'd better see a doctor.''

I leaned against the Chevrolet's rear fender and figured out what I wanted to say. The rain had almost completely stopped now, and in the silence I could hear a bird making small complaining sounds in the cottonwood. The nearest house in sight was well over a block to the north, which—together with the lateness of the hour—explained why the crash hadn't brought out a crowd. A block to the south the faint sound of a car motor rose, faded and died abruptly.

I said, "Where've you been hiding out, Mr. Wirtz?''

He just shook his head and stared at the blood on his handkerchief.

"Can't you get it through your head I know what I'm talking about? You're in hot water, mister. Four different people are interested in you because of that manuscript. And the cops want you for a pair of murders.''

Nothing showed in his face that hadn't been there before. He said, "You still haven't told me anything,'' in an emotionless voice.

At least I had unpried his jaws. I said, "Well, the Bishop, for one. And a man named Myles Benbrook—although you know more about that than I do. Also, an old hoodlum with death in his throat. Number four is a somebody you and I haven't met yet, and lucky for us we haven't: a somebody named Jafar Baijan.''

He stood there, rubbing his hands nervously together around the handkerchief, a weary slump to his thin shoulders. He said, "How do you know all these things?''

"I'll tell you that. I'm not a city cop, Mr. Wirtz; I'm

a private investigator named Pine and I was hired by the
Bishop to bring you back to him with that manuscript.
I know you've been afraid to go back there because the
cops wanted to question you about the body in your
closet. But that was nothing to the way they want you
now—since you put a knife in that sergeant early yesterday morning.''

His shoulders jerked. ''I haven't killed anyone, Mr.—
Mr. Pine.''

''Good! I'm delighted to hear you say so. But the
buttons are the ones you'll have to convince. Not me.''

''The police haven't any proof that I killed him.''

''Pardon me. They do have. In large amounts and
twenty-four carat. I'd like to make a suggestion, Mr.
Wirtz.''

He just looked at me.

''Let's drive over and pick up this manuscript, then
run up and deliver it to His Grace. We'll have to pick
up a man on the way, but he's a man who's on your
side. In fact you'll get your money a lot quicker because
of this man. Not twenty-five million bucks, though—I
think you realize you'll never get your hands on that kind
of money.''

''No!'' He almost shouted the word. ''I won't do it!
I don't trust you. You—you're lying to me.''

I shrugged. ''Okay. Get behind the wheel of my car.
We're going for a ride.''

He shrank away in quick alarm. ''No! I won't do it.
I don't have to go with you—anywhere.''

I moved the gun around in my hand. ''You'll go,
brother. Either to pick up that manuscript and deliver it
to the Bishop, or downtown to Central Station where the
boys in hard hats can bat you around on the Tinney
murder. Which will it be?''

He was trying to see past my expression. ''You mean
you'd actually turn me over to the police?''

''Uh-hunh.''

His chin came up. "Very well. Go ahead and do it!"

I blew out my breath slowly. Either he was calling my bluff or he was afraid of me enough to think he'd be safer with the cops. I hoped it was the former, for I had no intention at all of giving him to the Homicide boys.

Either way, it left it up to me to call *his* bluff. Maybe by the time we got within sight of Central Station he would reconsider.

I said, "It's your choice, Mr. Wirtz. Let's go."

We turned and started for the Plymouth. And in that moment a shadow flickered from behind the wrecked coupe. I started to whirl around while lifting my gun. Something came down on the back of my head and simultaneously I felt the gun torn from my fingers.

The pavement reached slowly up and laid itself against my left cheek. I heard a hoarse cry from a man's throat and four dim hammer beats turned to faraway bells.

Then nothing. Nothing at all.

# · 11 ·

It had started to rain again. I could feel drops against a cheek and my hair and on the back of one hand. Small drops and cool, with an uneven breeze blowing them in against me. . . .

I opened my eyes slowly and looked along a stretch of shining black asphalt that started somewhere in the neighborhood of my left ear and went on out into infinity. The heavy throbbing I could hear must have been my heart. I wondered fuzzily how it had managed to get shoved up into the back of my head. I decided after a while that the view wasn't really exceptional and that I should get up and go about my business.

By the time I managed to roll over and get one knee under me, it was time to sleep some more. I hung there like a dog with the colic and swung my head back and forth. Give me a full moon, I thought, and I'll bay at it.

I pushed hard against the pavement with both palms . . . and came up on my feet.

Wirtz's wrecked coupe was still half over the curb, right in front of me. And a lucky thing. By grabbing the rear fender I was able to keep the street away from my face.

After I stood there a while, my fingers chewing the fender and the rain beating against my head, I felt strong enough to lift my arm and look at the strap watch. Two-twelve. An hour and twenty-five minutes since I picked Wirtz up at the garage.

Quite a guy—Wirtz. I had certainly scared him. I wondered what it was he had hit me with. And then I recalled that flickering shadow from behind the car. Wirtz wasn't the one who had sapped me.

What had happened to Wirtz?

I turned around . . . and the question was answered. The tall slender man in the gray topcoat lay flat on his back in the center of the street, his head only inches from the Plymouth's left front wheel, his arms flung wide in a last gesture of defiance. A hell of a lot of good being defiant had done him. Even with little light and my eyes bleary from shock I could see he was dead.

But I went over there anyway. It took some doing and my stomach tried twice to pole-vault up behind my sternum. But I made it. I'll always be proud of that.

Four bullet holes, spaced untidily between his right shoulder and his left thigh. One through the chest and one in the belly. The one in his chest had either pierced his heart or come very close to it, judging from the position of the hole and lack of blood around it.

Not good shooting, but effective just the same. Panic behind the trigger but the bullets didn't care. End of the trail for Mr. Wirtz. "Good morning, Mr. Smith. Do you have a book for me to read?"

I walked slowly to the corner and looked at the words on a signpost. Corner of Central Avenue and Dakin Street. A long way from where the chase had started. But not too far to discourage the boys who would want to hear about it.

I went back to my car and set out to find a phone.

I sat behind the wheel of the Plymouth and watched raincoated men from three cars go over the street and its parkways with pocket torches while two police photographers set off flashbulbs that lit up the night like an electrical storm. The body still spreadeagled the pavement and the wrecked Chevvy sagged against the cottonwood like an old drunk.

It was three-forty-five in the morning. The rain had

stopped again to catch its breath, but there was still a chill mist hanging in the air. I slumped deeper in the seat and massaged the back of my head with gentle fingers. Even gentle fingers felt like a flame-tipped rake. The second time in less than thirty-six hours. How long could a head last?

At four-ten a uniform man from an Austin district prowl car opened my door. "Time to go, mister," he said in a flat unfriendly voice. "I'll ride along to make sure you don't get lost."

"Well, wipe your feet before you put them in here."

He gave me a blank glare and climbed in next to me, grunting a little. I started the motor and let out the clutch. Two of the other cars were already out of sight; the third was probably waiting for the meat wagon. As I made the turn, a tow truck came around the corner, its hoist chains rattling.

What with the hour and clear streets all the way, I made very good time. But when I finished parking around the corner from the Austin station and went in, the boys from Central Homicide were waiting for me.

We went along a narrow corridor with splotched brown walls and into a fair-sized oblong room where there were straight-backed chairs, a flat-topped pine table with cigarette burns around its edges, and chill bare walls the same ugly color as those outside. Hard white light streamed down from two inverted bowls of frosted glass, each on three brass chains from the ceiling.

They let me sit down on one of the chairs, probably because I looked as bad as I felt. The man in charge was Lieutenant Overmire, just as it had been exactly twenty-four hours before. A different station house, a different room, a different body to talk about. But I was still catching for the losing team.

Overmire was still lean, still soft-spoken. I thought his dark hair seemed a little grayer at the temples, but that couldn't have been true. He had on the same suit and maybe the same shirt, but this time the bow tie was a dark green.

One other change: where yesterday his eyes had been chill, today they were colder than the ice cubes in Connie Benbrook's Scotch.

He swung a leg over one corner of the table and bent forward far enough to let me see his eyes, while the three men with him found chairs somewhere behind me. "Tell me about it, Pine."

"It goes along with yesterday's story, Lieutenant. Only this time I found Wirtz. I tailed him, hoping to locate his cave. He made me and tried to throw me off with some fancy driving. He tried too hard and smashed a wheel. I hate to tell you the finish because you're not going to believe it."

"Try me."

"I was going to bring him in. To Headquarters."

"What detained you?"

"I was hit on the head."

"By Wirtz?"

"No. By whoever shot him. The shooting came after I was hit."

"Who pulled the trigger?"

"I don't know. I was hit from behind."

"Any idea who could have done it?"

"Not enough of an idea to talk out loud about."

"Still dealing them from your hip pocket, is that it?"

"No, Lieutenant." I was sweating now. "I haven't a thing that's solid enough to build a dream castle on."

"Let me be the judge of that."

I didn't say anything.

Overmire clasped his hands over a bent knee and rocked himself gently, still cold in the eyes. "Three deaths, Pine. By violence. Murders, my friend. And with you right in the middle of every one of the three."

I didn't say anything—again.

"I'm going to lock you up, Pine. I'm going to hold

you until I get out of you the name that goes with this idea of yours. Now, tell me I can't get away with it.''

More silence. Abruptly he got off the desk corner, went over to the door and out. I yawned, getting a thrust of pain through my battered head. One of the men behind me cleared his throat with a harsh sound and I jumped, adding to the pain.

The door opened and Lieutenant Overmire was with us again, carrying a bunched white cloth which sagged in the middle. He put it down on the table and turned back its corners, revealing a thin gold-filled cigarette case and lighter to match, an open-faced watch in what appeared to be platinum, keys on a chain, a brown leather wallet, a handkerchief with a few smears of blood on it, three business-size envelopes with neatly slit edges, and the ball-point pen I had come across while frisking Wirtz for a gun.

Overmire dragged a chair around behind the table, facing me, and began to finger through the collection, his face expressionless. None of the stuff held him for long until he came to the envelopes and wallet. He took his time about going through them.

Finally he shoved everything aside and leaned his elbows on the table and looked at me over locked fingers. ''Tonight was the first time you met Wirtz?''

''Yeah.''

''Where did you first pick him up?''

In a few words I told him about remembering Wirtz's car and how I had gone about locating it. He nodded thoughtfully a time or two when I finished.

''Another thing you didn't tell us. I'm surprised at you, Pine. I really am.''

''Well, don't be,'' I said, beginning to get angry. ''My job was to find Wirtz and I was working at it. You suspected him of being a killer but that doesn't mean he was one. I'm not working for you boys; I wasn't then and I'm not now. I have to do things the way I think they should be done. I don't break any laws, but I'm not a Department pigeon, either.''

I sounded a little scared, even to my own ears.

He sighed. The detective business was a hard job for him, even though he was good at it. He said, ''Why did he try to run away from you?''

''Because he had something hidden away that other people wanted. He thought I was one of them.''

''After he piled up his car, you talked with him?''

''Only a few words.''

''What about?''

''I told him who I was, that the Bishop wanted to know why he had failed to keep his original appointment. I asked where he'd been hiding out and where was the manuscript. I didn't get any answers.''

''What else?''

''Nothing else. I pointed my gun at him and said to get in my car. We started over there and the roof fell in. Did you find my gun?''

''There was an unfired .38 under his body.'' He stood up and came around the desk and bent down until his face was close to mine, his gray eyes colder than ever. ''You're lying to me, Pine. Not only lying but being clumsy about it. Did you honestly think it would stay covered up or are you just playing for time, hoping to get out of here long enough to finish the job you were hired to do?''

I sat there and looked back at him and said nothing at all.

He said heavily, ''Are you going to insist that you didn't know the dead man's name was Myles Benbrook?''

The complete astonishment in my expression was his answer. Some of the frostiness left his eyes and he said, ''You really didn't know that, did you?'' in an almost gentle voice. He straightened and leaned back against the table.

"No," I said. "I didn't know it. I'm not sure I know it now."

"When you talked to him, did he tell you his name was Wirtz?"

"Not in so many words, no. He was driving Wirtz's car, his description fitted the very weak and very general one I had of Wirtz, and our conversation was along lines only Wirtz could have understood. I called him Wirtz; not to have called him that would have been like a man asking his wife if she was married."

Overmire reached around and picked up the leather wallet. "This came out of the dead man's pocket, Pine. Filled with all kinds of identification in the name of Myles Benbrook, including a driver's license complete with picture."

He flopped the wallet up and down on the back of his left hand. "I called his home out on Sheridan Road and talked to his wife. She said Benbrook has been missing for the last four days. I sent a car out to pick her up."

I said, "Then you must have known he was Benbrook before going through that business of looking through his papers just now."

The phone on the table rang once. He put down the wallet and took up the receiver. "Overmire."

He listened, said, "Yes," listened some more and said, "Bring her in here." He hung up slowly and raised his eyebrows at me. "The wife identified him. Let's hear what she has to say."

A harness cop opened the door and Constance Benbrook, in lusterless black silk, a white spring coat over one arm, came in. There was grief in her face, but not a great deal of grief. Her face seemed whiter than I last remembered it, and in the harsh glare of light from overhead I saw a wrinkle or two that were new to me but not to her.

Overmire had introduced himself with the gravity the situation called for and she was seated before she saw me as something more than just another pair of pants. Surprise widened her brown eyes and she said, "You!" almost shrilly.

Overmire's neck was stiff as a pointer's. "So you two know each other." His tone said he was going to make something of it.

I said, "Mrs. Benbrook hired me to find her husband."

In the sudden brittle silence I took out my cigarettes and lighted one. Lieutenant Overmire waited until I blew out the match and dropped it on the floor. A lot of thoughts were milling around behind those cold eyes.

"And you found him, I see," he said at last. "I must really be slipping. I believed your little act when I threw Benbrook's name at you. Never again, Pine."

I said, "Stop sounding like I deflowered you, for Chrisakes. Mrs. Benbrook called on me later the same day I went to work for Bishop McManus. She'd seen my name in the paper as the one who found Post's body in Wirtz's room. Benbrook was an old friend of Wirtz's and he disappeared the same day. The answer to why is simple: he found Wirtz a hide-out until an opportunity came to get the manuscript to the Bishop. Hotels or rooming houses wouldn't do, so he hid him out in a private home.

"I'll go a ways further, while I'm at it. Up until you showed me Benbrook was the latest corpse, instead of Wirtz, I had me a theory. I would have given six, two and even that Myles Benbrook was the killer of Willie Post and Sergeant Frank Tinney."

"You filthy, filthy liar!" Constance Benbrook was out of her chair, all the loveliness gone from her face, her hands red-tipped claws. "I'll—I'll——"

Overmire waved her back to her chair. "Finish it up, Pine."

"He wanted that manuscript," I said. "These two men weren't such great friends that Benbrook would be willing to risk an accessory rap on friendship alone. Take that motivation away from him and greed is the only one left. Wirtz had told him when he, Wirtz, intended to make his first call on the Bishop. In Wirtz's absence from the room on Erie Street, Benbrook went there to hunt for the manuscript. Post walked in on him and got himself knifed.''

''Why did Post walk in there in the first place?''

''To get the manuscript himself. It must be clear to you by now that that hunk of paper, or whatever it is, is very valuable. Crooks can smell out valuables like that further than a cop can smell free drinks.''

Overmire flushed, started to yell at me, coughed instead and said, ''How do you tie Tinney's murder to Benbrook?''

''Both men died with a toothpick through the heart. Considering everything else, it means the same killer did both jobs. When Wirtz called the Bishop, he said, during the conversation, there was only one man in Chicago he trusted and he was beginning to have his doubts about that one. He must have meant Benbrook; there's no other way to figure it.

''Wirtz arranges to meet me at a certain street corner. To Benbrook, delivery of the manuscript to me means his chance of getting it himself is gone. Wirtz, we'll say—and there are excellent reasons for saying it—Wirtz doesn't have the script with him when he goes out to meet me. Benbrook follows him, expecting to see Wirtz take me to where it is hidden. But instead of me showing up, a policeman—Tinney—steps out of the shadows and tells Wirtz he's under arrest. Actually, I suppose, Tinney had located Wirtz's hide-out, wasn't sure Wirtz was inside and waited until the guy came out to nab him. When Tinney saw his man sneak out of the house to keep an appointment with me, he tailed Wirtz to the selected corner before attempting an arrest.

''Benbrook, watching from the shadows, realizes Wirtz's arrest will ruin his own hope of getting the manuscript, and so he kills Tinney. Then he and Wirtz run back to their hide-out.''

I stopped there, waiting for comments. Overmire was chewing a thumbnail and looking vaguely at the floor. Constance Benbrook was red in the face and hating me to pieces. One of the plain-clothes men behind me somewhere shuffled his feet on the linoleum and cleared his throat.

Lieutenant Overmire said, ''That's your theory, Pine?''

''Uh-hunh. Or rather it *was* my theory. But now that Benbrook himself has been knocked off, it isn't so good any more. The new theory now is that Wirtz killed all three men: first, Post when he found him in his apartment; second, Tinney for trying to arrest him; third, Benbrook because he was afraid I was going to take him, Benbrook, to the police and the guy might tell where the killer was hiding out.''

Overmire rubbed the sides of his forehead between the thumb and fingers of his left hand, a gesture of infinite weariness. He looked up and around to where Connie Benbrook sat fuming. ''Have you anything to say that may throw some light on this matter, Mrs. Benbrook?''

''You bet I have!'' she snarled. ''Of all the insane, insulting, vile lies I ever heard! He's just trying to throw blame on a wonderful man who is dead now and can't defend——''

''I mean,'' Overmire said smoothly, ''anything we can use, Mrs. Benbrook. Something, for instance, that might tell us where Raymond Wirtz is hiding out.''

Her teeth came together like the jaws of a bear trap. ''I have nothing to say to you,'' she said coldly.

The lieutenant thought about her answer. At least he appeared to be thinking about it. ''The man will take you home now, Mrs. Benbrook. Thanks for allowing me to intrude on your grief even this much. I'll notify you about the inquest and whatever else you will have to be bothered about.''

Without a word she stood up and stalked over to the

door. There she turned back to say, "My—my husband's body. What will—?"

"The coroner's office will call you, Mrs. Benbrook."

I got myself skewered on those brown eyes, then she was gone. I had had my last drink of Connie Benbrook's Scotch and my last taste of her lipstick. Twin blows that I would manage to survive.

"Well, Pine?" Overmire was watching me without expression.

I said, "I'm tired and my head hurts and I'm through talking. I'm going to bed, either in my own apartment or in one of your cells. I don't give a good goddam which."

He took a full minute to make up his mind. "Go on home, Pine. But stay where I can find you when the time comes. No trips out of town."

I said bitterly, "There goes my vacation in Upper Mongolia!" I stood up, jammed my hat over the undamaged side of my head and went out the door.

# ·12·

A buzzing in my ears pulled me up and out of dark depths. I opened my eyes after a while and looked at the ceiling. White calcimine, with a small dark spot near one corner where I killed a wasp the summer before. The buzzing stopped suddenly.

I turned my head on the pillow and looked through the slats of the Venetian blind. Still cloudy but I couldn't see any rain dropping past the glass. Right away I felt slightly better. I was tired of rain.

The buzzing started again. It seemed very loud now and I realized it wasn't in my head at all but coming from the door buzzer. I got up, staggering a little, said a bitter word, and went into the living room to open the door.

It was Lola North—Mrs. Lola Wirtz, rather. She blinked up at me and said, "My! What cute pajamas!" She looked cool and fresh and young, wearing a Pliofilm raincoat over a tailored blouse in pale yellow and a brown-and-white hound's-tooth suit that couldn't have been as expensive as it looked.

"Come in," I said, not being cordial about it. I closed the door and watched her draw up the two Venetian blinds and open a window before shrugging out of the raincoat and placing it on the radiator.

She turned around and gave me a pert grin. Not a care in the world. She said, "Not that you don't look impossibly virile in them, but why not get out of those pajamas and into some clothing? It's after one o'clock, you know. In the afternoon.''

"I was sleeping," I growled. "I had a bad night and my head hurts and I don't feel like entertaining lovely young women. I don't even feel like entertaining ugly old women.''

"And grouchy, too!" Her smile faded. "You don't look good at that. Your eyes are all bloodshot and dark circles under them.''

"I've got a hole in the back of my head, too. Do you know how to make coffee?''

"Of course.''

"Then go make some.''

She went into the kitchen. I spent fifteen minutes showering, shaving and brushing my teeth. The back of my head was still sore but nothing I wouldn't get over in time. I wondered how much time I had before somebody else tried to take a swing at the same spot.

Lola North had cups, saucers and a pot of coffee in the center of the breakfast table and was dropping bread into the toaster as I came into the kitchen. She gave me an approving glance. "That's better. Sit down while I go around being wifely.''

The kiss she'd given me two nights before must have done more for her than it had for me. I found some brandy behind a can of pretzels in the pantry and poured a slug into my cup and coffee over that. I drank almost half without stopping, burning my tongue and gullet. But the warmth spread through me, and by the time I filled the cup a second time I was ready to talk.

"Anything special behind this call?" I asked. "Or is this your morning for good works in the parish?''

Her eyes were innocent over the rim of her cup. "I phoned your office around eleven. When nobody answered, I bet myself you were just lying around in bed. So I came over to find out.''

"Uh-hunh. Now the real reason. Your casual air stinks.''

"Why, Paul!"

"The real reason, hey?"

Abruptly she sobered. "Something has happened. Have you seen the afternoon papers?"

"In my sleep?"

"Of course; that was silly." The toaster popped, giving her a chance to avoid my eyes while she buttered two slices. "When we talked on the way home from that—that man's, you mentioned that a Myles Benbrook, here in Chicago, was a friend of Raymond's."

"I talk too much," I growled.

The knife clattered against the butter plate, and her eyes came up to mine. "Myles Benbrook was murdered last night, Paul. He was found shot to death beside a wrecked car out in the west end of town." She took a deep unsteady breath. "Paul, it was Raymond's car!"

"No! Pass the toast."

She was mad at me. "Aren't you listening? Don't you realize what this may mean?"

"Certainly I do." I took a slice of toast and bit gingerly into it. "It may mean your precious mild little old husband has run the score up to three corpses."

"Three? I——"

"Sorry. I forgot Overmire kept the Wirtz angle out of the papers on number two. There was a cop stabbed to death early yesterday morning out on Sacramento. I was supposed to meet your husband out there, but he had to run along before I showed up. So's not to disappoint me entirely, he left me a fresh body. For laughs, I guess."

She bit her lips and bent her head. "I—I can't believe it. He was always so . . . gentle. So completely without violence. What could have changed him this way?"

"How do I know? Maybe greed, Mrs. Wirtz. May I call you Lola? Greed born in him when you walked out because he was gentle and without violence—and therefore without money. You have to be a violent person to make money. I don't necessarily mean the stab-and-shoot kind of violence. I mean the kind that will let you kick other people aside to get your hands dipped in gold. Am I boring you? I am me.''

I picked up the pot and refilled my cup and hers. It had started to rain again; I could hear it at the windows.

I said, ''It may be your husband hasn't killed anyone. I wouldn't say that except for one thing: the international crook Louie Antuni mentioned. You know, this Jafar Baijan character. The fact that he hasn't looked me up yet means either that he doesn't know I'm in the middle of the whole mess—which hardly seems likely—or he's decided I'm not important enough to bother with. If there is a Jafar Baijan at all.''

She said with abrupt intensity, ''We've got to find Raymond, Paul. We've got to find him immediately. If he hasn't killed anyone, he must go to the police and tell them so.''

''And if he has?''

She only shook her head and looked away from me.

I said, ''I went out to a place yesterday where he might be. No one was home, so I'm going out there again today. Would you like to come along?''

Her hand jumped out and caught one of mine, almost upsetting my cup. ''Paul! You've found him! Do you think he still has—?''

''Uh-hunh,'' I said, giving her a one-sided grin. ''The manuscript, hey? Poor, dear Raymond. Surprising how much compassion twenty-five million bucks will buy, isn't it?''

She couldn't meet my eyes. ''You're wrong! I didn't mean——''

''Sure you did. I'm a cynical old man, Mrs. Wirtz; try being anything else in my business.''

''It's just that I don't want him victimized by——''

The buzzer at the corridor door sounded briefly. Lola Wirtz and I sat there and looked at each other in the sudden silence.

"Who do you think it is?" she whispered, wide-eyed.

I got up. "Probably the vice squad. This will teach you a lesson about going to men's apartments."

I left her sitting there and went into the living room, opening the door just as the buzzer went off again. It was Lieutenant Overmire of the Homicide Detail, in a gray suit and bow tie, blue this time, and looking as fit and rested as I didn't.

He gave me a polite smile with no warmth in it and glanced past me into my living room. I blocked the opening and gave him the raised eyebrow and said, "Was there something, Lieutenant?"

His gaze was fixed on something beyond my right shoulder. "That's a nice handbag on your table. Am I interrupting something?"

"Oh, come on in, for Chrisakes!" I stepped aside and he went past me and took off his gray hat and rotated it gently between his fingers while his chill eyes took in the blue and beige couch, the blue tapestry of the easy chair, the bookcase, the pictures on the wall, the sand-colored carpeting. His eyes stopped when they reached Lola North standing in the kitchen doorway.

I said, "Miss North, this is Lieutenant Overmire, a Homicide detective."

He gave her a nicer smile than I had thought he carried in stock. "Sorry to break in this way, Miss North."

I said, "What's on your mind, Lieutenant. I'd like to get back to my breakfast. Would you like some coffee?"

"No. I thought you might like to know that we've located Wirtz's hide-out."

The gasp was Lola North's. But my jaw was hanging too. "That's fine. Case all wrapped up now, hunh? Good work, Lieutenant."

He looked from me to her and back to me again, his eyes still chill and his expression not saying anything. "I'm afraid not. No. He left there two nights ago, it seems. I've had men combing the neighborhood where

Tinney's body was found. This morning, after Benbrook was found to be mixed in the case, one of my men located his former secretary, a woman named Irene Taylor. It seems she was—very close to Benbrook and had been for years. He brought Wirtz there five days ago and left him to hide out in that house until the morning Tinney was killed. The Taylor woman claimed she didn't know Wirtz was a fugitive, and, of course, there's no way to check that now. She insists she hasn't seen either man during the past two days and has no idea where Wirtz is now. I think she's telling it straight: that Benbrook used her and that's all. She didn't seem particularly upset at news of his death, and that surprised me a little, considering what they'd meant to each other.''

"More fun," I said meaninglessly.

The three of us stood there and looked at one another and said nothing. The silence was getting a little uncomfortable when Overmire said, "I thought you'd like to know, Pine. I'd hoped maybe telling you would jog your memory."

"Believe me, Lieutenant, I'm completely at sea."

"All right. You know where to find me. Good-by, Miss North, it was nice meeting you."

He went out, closing the door softly at his back. I sighed a big sigh and went back into the kitchen to my cooling coffee.

Lola North followed me in and sat down across from me. "Does it mean anything, Paul?"

"Quite a bit—none of it important. It means policemen are smart and have an organization, it means Wirtz is beyond finding until something stirs him up again, it means the lead I thought I had is as dead as Benbrook."

"What lead?"

"You heard the man, Miss North. What I told you just before he came in. The place I went out to yesterday was Irene Taylor's home. Sure enough, Wirtz had been there and is no longer. I'm right back where I was the day Bishop McManus hired me."

I drank some coffee moodily and looked out the kitchen window. The rain was still pouring it on. Another couple of days and we'd all be building arks.

"What are you going to do now, Paul?"

"Go down to my office and sit. I'm expecting a telegram that won't help me at all, and I've got a book to finish. Then I'm going to sit there and think. It's time I did some of both."

"How late will you be there?"

"How do I know?" I looked at her blonde hair, at her beautiful blue eyes, at her troubled expression. "Days, maybe. Thinking has always been a chore for me. Somewhere in all this tangle is something I've missed and had no business missing. Once my fat head puts my fat hand on it the works will begin to unravel. But don't hold your breath until then."

"Could I come along with you? I mean we could sit there and talk it over and over until you see what you're after."

"Nope." I drained my cup and got up. "But thanks anyway. Now where'd I put my hat?"

I found it on the radiator in the bathroom and put on my trench coat. Downstairs, I said, "I'm going to the Loop. Can I drop you somewhere?"

"No, thank you." She sounded distant and a little hurt. "I'll manage. Could I call you at the office later?"

"Do that."

I left her there and ran down the street, through the rain, to where the Plymouth waited.

# · 13 ·

It took longer than usual to get downtown, just as it always does when the streets are wet. The upper stories of Loop skyscrapers were hidden by low-hanging clouds and a mixture of smoke and fog, and offices and display windows were lighted. There was a line of cars waiting to get into the parking lot and it was fifteen minutes before I could get rid of mine.

At three-ten I unlocked the inner office door. A yellow envelope lay on the floor under the letter drop and I scooped it up. A Western Union night letter from Los Angeles. The answer to my wire to Cliff Morrison. By this time probably not worth the paper it was pasted on.

I opened the blind and the window beyond that and sat down to learn about Raymond Wirtz.

RAYMOND FINLEY WIRTZ AGE 45 OWNS HOME 1217 HILLROSE WITH $4000 MORTGAGE. ASSISTANT PROFESSOR USC AND WELL-KNOWN PALEOGRAPHER. SEPARATED FROM WIFE FORMER LOLA NORTH NOW LIVING IN GLENDALE. WIRTZ LEFT LA MAY 2 THIS YEAR DRIVING GRAY CHEVROLET CLUB COUPE 41 MODEL LICENSE 7F26-419 DESTINATION UNKNOWN. RETURN EXPECTED AS HOUSE IS NOT FOR SALE. NO POLICE RECORD AND NEIGHBORS REGARD HIM AS OKAY. MARRIAGE LASTED ONE YEAR. NO REPORT OF OTHER MAN AS REASON AL-

THOUGH WIFE SAID TO BE TYPE WHO LIKED
PARTIES AND NIGHTCLUBS WHILE WIRTZ WAS
FIRESIDE AND SLIPPERS MAN. SHALL WE DIG
INTO HER FOR YOU QUESTION MARK. COME
TO SUNNY CALIFORNIA. BILL FOLLOWS. BE
SURE YOU PAY IT.

                                   CLIFF

Nothing in it but a better picture of Lola North Wirtz. Too old for her, she had said. But not too old for her to hunt him up when he was in trouble, her face and voice filled with compassion and her heart filled with dollar signs. That was her business and his, and no affair of mine.

I dug out the McGivern mystery novel and finished it over half a pack of cigarettes. The women in it were beautiful and the private eye was brilliant. I would have liked to be brilliant, too. I would even have liked to be reasonably intelligent. I put the book away.

I loosened my tie and got out of my coat. I walked up and down the floor. I sat down. I stood up again and went over to the window. Nothing out there that wasn't there yesterday and wouldn't be there tomorrow. I walked up and down the floor. I kicked the wastebasket. I wished I had a bottle in my bottom drawer. I lighted a cigarette and stared long and hard at the calendar girl.

I went out and bought a bottle.

The liquor bit into my intestines like it enjoyed the job. I put my heels on the desk blotter and thought over everything I'd done and heard and said from the minute I had first walked through those rectory doors.

Nothing came out of it. Looking at it from a strictly logical viewpoint, there was no mystery at all. Wirtz had come to Chicago to sell something, told a friend about it, and the friend went into action by killing two men, then getting killed himself by Wirtz. And somewhere Wirtz was hiding until memories cooled enough to let him stick his nose out as far as the rectory. Then he could turn the manuscript over to the Bishop, sell the Bishop on the idea that he, Wirtz, wasn't a killer but just the victim of a frame, then hide out long enough for the twenty-five million to come through. With that kind of money he could hire lawyers who would go into court and prove their client wouldn't have killed a boll weevil to save his cotton.

I thought of Connie Benbrook. I thought of Lola North Wirtz. I thought of Gypsy Rose Lee. Whatever had become of her?

I walked the floor some more. I went to the bathroom down the hall. I came back and bought myself another drink.

Five-thirty, according to my wrist watch. I didn't believe it and put it against my ear. Still ticking, still spewing out wasted seconds.

I sat down and went through the whole case again. I got the same answer and a still stronger sense of futility. I had me another drink.

The phone rang. Lola North Wirtz was on the other end. "Have you got anything, Paul?" She sounded anxious.

"Leprosy. Go away."

"What's the matter with you? Are you all right?"

"No. Where are you?"

"At home—the Lake Towers." She sounded expectant now.

"Stay there," I said and hung up.

Ten minutes later I went out for dinner.

When I came out of the restaurant the rain had stopped again. I walked north on Wabash Avenue, away from the office, then west on Randolph and into a movie without looking to see what was listed on the marquee. It turned out to be something about dancing girls and a beautiful princess of the Far East and a handsome vagabond who sang about love. In color. I enjoyed every minute of it. The second feature was about a moody blind piano teacher who fell in love so hard he got his sight back and played his own symphony in Carnegie Hall and got Beethoven's old job as a reward. I could have sat through it twice. Just as long as it wasn't about a brilliant private detective.

I came out at ten-fifteen. It was raining again. I went into a restaurant and read a morning paper while drinking four cups of coffee. I made up my mind to go back and get my car and go home and the hell with it.

At ten-fifty I was back in the office with my heels on the blotter and the bottle in my lap, starting all over again.

I tried to figure out how Wirtz had been able to follow Benbrook and me all the way out to where Benbrook was killed. It didn't make sense that he would send Benbrook to pick up the Chevvy at the garage, then tail him to make sure he did a good job of it.

That got me to thinking about Benbrook. A businessman—at least a former businessman. Businessmen were usually methodical. Now what?

I went back to that wild chase through Chicago streets. Where had Benbrook been going? To join Wirtz at a new hide-out; that seemed plain enough. But he'd spotted me before he could lead me there. My mistake was sticking too close to his heels when he turned off Kedzie at Addison. Benbrook hadn't wanted Addison; that's why he doubled back and caught me. Maybe the next street north was the one he had wanted. Benbrook was a methodical man. . . .

And right then is when I turned out to be a detective.

I put the bottle on the desk with great care and slowly lowered my feet to the floor. I began to dig through the pockets of my coat. Was this the suit I had worn yesterday afternoon? I couldn't remember.

It wasn't necessary to remember. A sheet of paper, folded twice, came out into the light. The list of names

and addresses I had copied from those papers in Benbrook's private strongbox.

I spread it flat on the blotter and read each entry with
slow care. Number six was my baby. Clear and shining
and filled with promise. I read the words aloud, with
only my ears to hear them.

"William L. Snyder, 3309 West Grace Street."

Grace Street. Three blocks from where Benbrook spotted me and began to run.

I dug out the phone book, looked up a number and
called it. Mrs. Benbrook has retired; there's been a death
in the family. I'm so sorry to hear that, but this is very
important, please call her to the phone. The hell you
won't, brother! Get her on the wire before I pull you in
for barratry!

Three minutes later an extension receiver went up.
"Who is this?" Connie Benbrook, and angry too.

"Paul Pine, Mrs. Benbrook. I——"

"Well, you certainly have a nerve! Bothering me at
a time like this."

I said, "Does the name William L. Snyder mean anything to you, Mrs. Benbrook?"

It surprised the anger out of her. "Who? Snyder? I
don't . . ." Her voice died out, then came back sharp
and clear. "You mean Bill Snyder, Myles's friend at the
steel company?"

"That's the guy."

"Why, Bill's in Europe—has been for a month. I have
no idea when he'll be back. Why do you ask?"

"Just a routine check, Mrs. Benbrook. Sorry I bothered you. Good night."

I laid the receiver back with care, took a quick and
stiff drink, put the bottle away and went over to the filing
cabinet. From the bottom drawer I took an underarm
holster and my Colt .38, put them where they belonged
and my suit coat on over them and my trench coat over
that. Ready for big game, with a smile on my lips and
a song in my heart.

I was halfway to the office door when I heard light fast feet crossing the reception room. I opened the door and there was Lola Wirtz.

She was dressed in the same outfit, the plastic raincoat glistening in the light from the office fixture. No smile, blue eyes serious and direct. "I was worried, Paul. I called and called and you didn't answer your phone."

"I was out. You're here just in time, Mrs. Wirtz. I have wonderful news for you—I think."

Her nostrils flared perceptibly under a quick breath. "What do you mean? Have you—have you . . . found him?"

"Possibly. I'm on my way to make sure."

"I'm coming with you!"

"I like family reunions," I said. "Come on then."

The theaters had just let out and there was a crowd at the parking lot waiting for cars. We waited almost twenty minutes before the Plymouth was brought down and turned over to me.

I took Michigan Avenue to the Drive and the Drive straight north to Addison before turning west. Lola Wirtz sat stiff and erect next to me, her eyes straight ahead, the fingers of both hands tight on the bag in her lap. The rain was a light mist now, just enough of it to make my windshield wipers necessary.

She was alone with her thoughts and I didn't try to break in on them. I rolled down a window an inch or two and sniffed at the night air and was pleased with myself.

Forty minutes of not sensational driving got us to the thirty-three hundred block on West Grace Street. It was a street of better than modest homes, brick mostly, with plenty of trees and shrubs here and there.

And there was a big black sedan parked in front of 3309.

I drove slowly past. There were lights in what I judged to be the living room, but the blinds were down. It seemed to be six rooms, maybe seven, all on one floor and set back from the street at the end of a shrub-lined walk. There was no one sitting in the black car and no one seemed to be standing around outside anywhere.

I parked on the same side of the street fifty or sixty feet farther west. To Lola Wirtz I said, "I'm wondering about that car. You stay here until I see if he has company."

She nodded without speaking. I got out and closed the door, being careful not to slam it, and walked back to the black sedan and peered in through the rain-smeared glass. Empty all right. I leaned against it and rubbed the point of my chin with my thumbnail and thought about going up there and ringing the bell.

While I was thinking about it, the lights in the living room winked out and a moment later the front door opened. I stepped quickly back and flattened myself against the sedan's opposite side.

The click of high heels came along the walk, almost running. I waited until I heard the car-door handle turn, then I stuck my head around and said, "Good evening, Mrs. Benbrook."

It was a hell of a thing to do. She went three feet into the air with shock and let out a sharp yelp that startled *me*. She reeled back and might have fallen if I hadn't caught her by one arm.

"Relax," I growled. "You're among friends."

"Paul!" She began to shiver uncontrollably. "You knew when you called me, didn't you? You knew he was here?"

"It seemed likely. And my bringing up Snyder's name that way got you to thinking along the same lines I had. Why did you come out?"

"I—— It doesn't matter. He's not in there now—if he ever was to begin with. I went through the entire house. Even the basement."

I said, "What's the matter with you? You're so scared you can hardly talk."

"You . . . startled me."

"You were scared before I even spoke to you. What did you find in there?"

"N-nothing. I told you that. Nothing at all. He's gone."

"I'll bet you forgot to look in the broom closet. Let's both try."

"No. I'm going home. It was a mistake for me to come here at all."

"Come on before I belt you one."

It sounded tough and it was meant to sound tough. She must have believed I meant every word of it too, for she went along the walk and up on the porch with me and no argument. The door was unlocked and I pushed it open, into darkness.

"You know where the switch is," I said. "Turn on the lights."

She reached around the door frame and an overhead light went on. It was a long wide hall that ran all the way back to a closed door, with other doors on either side along the way. The woodwork was in off-white enamel and there was gray wallpaper with a thin red stripe. A telephone stood on a small stand near a wide archway leading to the living room.

I closed the front door. "Very nice," I said. "So far anyway. Now let's try the living room."

She didn't move. She seemed to be listening to something not meant for human ears. I reached out and prodded her arm through the sleeve of her white coat and she turned her head and looked blankly at me.

"The living room," I said.

Tears began to squeeze out of her brown eyes and roll along her cheeks. She didn't look twenty-eight any more. Maybe she never again would look twenty-eight.

"He's dead, Paul."

"Uh-hunh. Number four. Where?"

"In there." She didn't point but I understood. "On the f-floor."

"You do it?"

She put a shaking hand against the base of her throat. Her eyes were wild. "No, no! I wouldn't—I found him——"

"Show me."

It ended up I was the one to find the light switch just inside the archway. Two bulbs glowed behind a pair of matching shields of frosted glass high on opposite walls. A long narrow room with gas logs in a small fireplace flanked by crowded bookshelves, a russet couch against one wall, lamp tables, two easy chairs, a built-in radio—all in blond wood.

Stretched out on the gray carpeting, face up, looking much too large in that position, was the twisted figure of a man.

He was fully dressed, except for a coat, and there was a trickle of blood along the left side of his face and a small pool of it soaking the carpet under his neck. A blue-edged hole about the circumference of a nickel pencil showed where a bullet had gone through his temple and into the brain. A .25 hand gun would have left a hole like that.

I knelt and put a hand against one cheek. Cooler than life but not yet as cold as old death. Dead not more than an hour and maybe much less.

I stood up and nodded for no particular reason. "How long were you in here, Mrs. Benbrook?"

"Less than five minutes." She said it quickly as though knowing in advance just what my first question would be.

"Did you bring a purse with you? A bag?"

That confused her. "It's in the car."

"Why did you come out here right after I called you?"

She shuddered and closed her eyes. "Must we stand here with this—this body in front of us, and discuss things? Have you no——"

"Don't give me that," I said nastily. "You could sit on his belly and eat your breakfast. You're tougher than

the sides of a battleship and we both know it. Why did
you come out here, Mrs. Benbrook?''

She turned abruptly and went back out into the hall
and sat down on the small chair next to the telephone
stand. I followed her out and leaned against the wall and
waited for my answer.

When she showed no indication of giving me one, I
said, "Let *me* tell *you*. You figured on getting that manuscript yourself. As Myles Benbrook's widow you'll come
into a fortune. But owning a fortune wouldn't keep you,
or anyone else, for that matter, from reaching out and
picking up another fortune if it was very easy to do.

"And this manuscript seemed to fill the bill. My guess
is that Benbrook told you all about the thing the day
Wirtz first came out to call on him. But it's only a guess
and not important because you heard enough about it
since then to know that Wirtz had it and it was incredibly
valuable.

"So, when I called you tonight, you did some quick
thinking and came up with the same answer I had: Raymond Wirtz was hiding out here. Your first thought was
of the manuscript and how to get hold of it. And the
answer was right there waiting for you. All you had to
do was run out here, tell Wirtz that unless he gave you
the thing, you would turn him over to the police. The
possibility of his killing you to prevent that was remote,
for you knew him well—you told me that yourself. You
knew him to be a quiet, unviolent man who probably
had killed no one and never would. Besides, by this time,
with bodies falling all around him, Raymond Wirtz was
probably sick to death of that manuscript and might drop
it in your lovely hand the minute you held it out in front
of him.

"So, out you came, ahead of me. Either you walked
in . . . How *did* you get in?"

Without looking at me, she said, "When no one answered my ring, I tried the door. It was unlocked.''

"Uh-hunh. Well, either you walked in and found Wirtz

dead on the rug or you put him there before you walked out. It's none of my business anyway, but it is police business and you'll be asked. Many times and many ways."

"I didn't kill him, Paul." She turned her face to me, a face haggard and tear-stained and full of fear. "You mustn't tell the police I was here. I couldn't bear . . . Don't tell them, Paul. I'll pay you. I'll pay you anything you ask!"

I said sourly, "Where would I spend it? This is my fourth corpse in three days. Par, Mrs. Benbrook, is one in a lifetime—if that. And each time I've had to stand in front of the Homicide boys and spread my empty hands and shrug my bent shoulders. This time, though, my hands aren't empty—I've got somebody to give them. You, Mrs. Benbrook."

No more fear in her face now. Fury, the kind of fury that would put claws at my throat in the next three seconds. Hatred, the kind of hatred that pulls triggers. The jungle looked at me out of those wild brown eyes and I stepped back one step.

A knock at the door.

The fury and hatred in that once lovely face disappeared under a new wave of fear and she was out of her chair like a shot and ready to run down the hall when I grabbed her arm. She turned on me, then, but weakly. All the strength was gone out of her.

I said, "Where you going to run to—Sioux City? Get a grip on yourself, for Chrisakes."

I left her standing there and went along the hall to the front door. It was Lola Wirtz, wonder in her face and a question on her lips. "Is—is everything all right, Paul?"

"Is anything ever right in this business? Come on in out of the rain."

She looked at Connie Benbrook standing near the phone, tears on her cheeks and terror in her eyes. "I don't want to intrude. . . ."

I took her by the arm, got her over the threshold and

closed the door. I said, "You won't like this, but I'm pretty sure it won't bust you wide open. There isn't going to be any family reunion, Mrs. Wirtz."

Behind me I heard Benbrook's widow make a small noise in her throat. Two widows in two days. You meet such interesting people.

"What do you mean, Paul?" Not worried, not frightened, just puzzled.

"Your husband is dead."

She closed her eyes, swallowed, opened them again. That was all. They come and they go, and besides he was too old for her. She had said so.

"I can't believe——" Voice clear enough but it did falter. "How do you know that?"

"He's in the living room. On the floor."

"Murdered?"

"Uh-hunh." I wondered bitterly if there was any other way to die.

"May—I see him?"

"It's your husband, all right. Mrs. Benbrook, here, identified him."

She looked at the older woman again and her jaw hardened just enough for me to notice. "How could she do that? I don't know her."

I said impatiently, "Do you want to look at him or don't you? I've got a phone call to make."

Her eyes flashed at that. "The police?"

"That's it. I bet they cheer me from the housetops." The words were sour against my tongue.

"What about that manuscript?"

I grinned. "Thanks, Mrs. Wirtz. You've saved my faith in human nature."

At the phone, I dialed Central Station and was put through to Homicide. Overmire was in, all right; without me he probably had little to do.

My lips seemed stiff as stone. "This is Paul Pine, Lieutenant."

"Pine?" Surprise filled his quiet voice. "Now what?"

"It's Wirtz this time. Murdered."

"You just won't learn, will you? All right. Where?"

"3309 Grace. It's a house. I'm calling from there."

"Don't go away." The crash against my left ear was his receiver going down.

# ·14·

After a while Lieutenant Overmire left the living room and came back into the hall. He said, "Let's use the kitchen," and we followed him toward the rear of the house and into a large-sized kitchen with ivory walls and the latest in modern equipment, all so clean and orderly it looked like a display window at the electric company.

There was a red-lacquered dinette set in a roomy breakfast nook to one side of a giant refrigerator. We sat down in there and Constance Benbrook and I lighted cigarettes after I found a saucer for ashes.

Overmire put his forearms against the table top and fixed his cold eyes on Lola Wirtz. He said, "I ought to question each of you separately. But you've had time enough to fix up a story you'll all use anyway. . . . Tell me your side of it, Miss North."

I said, "North is her maiden name, Lieutenant. This is Mrs. Raymond Wirtz."

"Oh?" His eyes stayed on her. "Why wasn't I told that when we met this afternoon, Mrs. Wirtz?"

Angry color burned in her cheeks. The anger was for me. "It wasn't important. I couldn't have told you anything about Raymond you didn't already know. We've been separated over a year now and I had absolutely no idea where he was hiding."

"What are you doing in town?"

She told him the story she had given me that night on the way home from Antuni's place. She bore down heavily on the compassion angle and Overmire believed it about as much as I had. He made no attempt to call her on it, however.

"All right, Mrs. Wirtz," he said when she was finished. "Now, how does it happen you came out here tonight?"

"I came out with Mr. Pine."

"What time did you get here?"

"A few minutes after midnight, I guess."

"You've been with Mr. Pine all evening?"

"No. I met him at his office around eleven o'clock."

"The two of you came right out here?"

"Yes."

He nodded once and dug a fountain pen from his breast pocket and a slip of paper from another. He asked her address and wrote it down and put paper and pen away. Then his frigid eyes nailed Connie Benbrook.

She was her old self again: younger than her years, her face made up and her smile working. She was as confident and at ease as a Mississippi congressman up for re-election. She was a widow with millions in the bank and a smooth story ready to tell: two things every cop would respect.

"When," Overmire said placidly, "did you get here, Mrs. Benbrook?"

"Almost exactly at midnight." No hesitation at all. "I noticed the car clock as I turned off the motor."

"Then you were here ahead of Mr. Pine and Mrs. Wirtz?"

"*Just* ahead of them. No more than two or three minutes."

"What caused you to come out here in the first place?"

She had an answer for that one, too. A nice smart quick answer, reasonable as you could want. If you were the gullible type.

"I hold a mortgage on this property, Lieutenant. When Mr. Pine unexpectedly called me around eleven o'clock and asked about the man who lives here, then hung up without an explanation, it . . . well, it worried me. I thought something might be wrong, a fire or something—so I came right out to see.''

''Umm,'' Overmire said and looked searchingly at his left thumb. ''What did you find?''

The hand holding the cigarette jerked a little and her smile faded. ''It wasn't pleasant. I saw that the house was dark and everything seemed to be in order. I found the door unlocked, turned on the hall light and was already a few steps into the living room before I saw the body. I turned on the light, recognized the dead man as Raymond Wirtz and ran out of the house. Mr. Pine was standing just outside the door.''

She made it sound as though I had just slipped Wirtz a bullet two minutes before and gone out to lurk in the shrubbery for more victims.

Overmire said dryly, ''Why didn't you call the police, Mrs. Benbrook? The phone was certainly handy enough.''

She bit her lip. ''I was afraid—terrified, Lieutenant. My only thought was to get out of this horrible place without a second's delay.''

Overmire's cold eyes came over to me. He wet his lips and said, ''Your turn, friend.''

I told him what I could: about getting the list from Mrs. Benbrook the day before, about checking against it to learn if any of Benbrook's property was in the vicinity of where he'd caught me tailing him, and about coming out here for that reason. It was such a reasonable and simple explanation that it sounded a little silly put into words, as the truth often does.

Overmire leaned back in his chair, hung his arm over its back and crossed his legs. ''I blame myself,'' he said quietly. ''I really do. Ever since I stepped into this case I've taken the easy way. A man named Wirtz had something to sell and he went around killing people who got in his way. It was just that simple, I told myself. Find

Raymond Wirtz and you've found the killer. No complications, no tangles, as easy as looking for a filling-station stick-up mob.

"But now Wirtz himself is dead and all that is changed." He ran a finger along the table edge and looked absently at it. "Either Wirtz did kill the first three, then was killed himself—or he murdered no one and the same person has four corpses to his credit. But that's only one side of it. What if this old manuscript—which no one I've talked to has ever actually seen—what if it isn't the real motive for these murders at all?"

He shook his head and sighed heavily and was silent for a long moment. Flash bulbs had stopped throwing brief bright flashes from the living room, but the Police Lab boys with their vacuum cleaners, tape measures and glassine envelopes were still at work in there.

He said, "Take the three stories I've just heard. Your husband has been dead only a few hours, Mrs. Benbrook, and you're a very wealthy woman. Yet you come running away out to the other end of town because you think maybe a house you own is on fire. And you, Mrs. Wirtz, you just happen to drop in at Pine's office exactly when he's starting out for the place your husband lies dead— murdered. . . . And you, Pine, sitting in your office thinking, when—bingo!—you know exactly where the man you've been hunting for days is hiding out. What's the matter with you people—you think the Department is full of nothing but idiots?"

I let out my breath gently and looked at the stricken faces of two beautiful women. Rain tapped an invitation at the windows, an invitation to come out and get soaked. Nothing would have made me happier.

"Well," Overmire growled, "I'm through coasting. I'm holding all three of you, and I'm going to keep on holding you just as long as I can make it stick. And you're going to get questioned, singly and together and over and over—until I can dig out of one of you some of the truth about this business that you're keeping from me.''

Constance Benbrook crushed her cigarette savagely into the saucer. "I can't speak for these two people, Lieutenant Overmire, but I'll tell you one thing. I know nothing at all about what's been going on and I'm not going to spend any time having policemen breathe in my face and yell a lot of nonsense in my ears. I'm going to call my attorney and I'm going to call him now. You don't frighten me even a little bit.''

Overmire's lips moved under a polite smile that seemed almost sad. He said, "We might as well get started," and began to rise from his chair.

I said, "Let me say something, Lieutenant.''

It got me stared at by the three of them. Overmire frowned. "This time you don't talk me out of it, Pine. I mean it.''

"I was given a job to do," I said, "and I muffed it. It happens to all of us, but this is one I didn't want to drop.''

I ground out my cigarette and lighted another and sat there turning the matchstick slowly between my fingers while I thought of what I wanted to say.

"Well," I said, "like it or not, I muffed it. And for the past three days now Bishop McManus has been holding a hand night and day on his phone, waiting for word from me that I've done the job he hired me to do. Getting that manuscript means more to him than anything else in the world, Lieutenant. Not alone for personal glory—although I'm sure bishops are human enough to want that too—but for what it would mean to the Church.''

Overmire shifted impatiently. "Get it over with, Pine. You're not saying anything.''

"I think I am. I'm saying I've loused up a job and that I'm entitled to make my report to my client, just as he's entitled to have his suspense ended one way or the other and without delay.''

"All right. Call him up and tell him. I don't object."

I shook my head. "I take my cases in person and I make my final reports the same way."

He thought about it for a long time, not really believing me, trying to guess what I was really after. Finally he nodded twice and his expression was knowing. "It won't work, Pine. You have a feeling he can talk me out of putting you through the wringer. Not a chance, friend."

I leaned back and slapped a hand down on my thigh. "Brother! You guys must have one hell of a union. You get so you even think alike. Okay, I'll give you an angle to look at, Lieutenant. Frankly it's about as weak as angles can get, so far off the beam I hate to throw it in at all."

Overmire perked up for the first time. Mention of an angle did that; he was where even the farfetched ones were welcome.

"Wirtz's killer got the manuscript tonight; otherwise he couldn't afford to kill him. But now that he's got it, what can he do with it? He's smart: he'll bury it until the heat dies, then turn it into cash. The Church will be his best bet, but not through the Bishop. Directly to Rome with it this time. That's the intelligent thing for him to do, the thing intelligent people will expect him to do."

Overmire said heavily, "You said something about an angle. I'd like to hear it."

"Sure. What if the guy does the one thing no one expects? What if he goes straight to the Bishop and makes his deal? *What if he's there right now?*"

There went the last of his respect for me. "Jesus! You call *that* an angle? The Bishop wouldn't touch the thing in these circumstances."

"I agree with you. I said this was away out of line when you think intelligently about it. So you throw it out, just as the killer figured you would. Thing is, Bishop McManus doesn't know Wirtz is dead. Nobody's supposed to know he's dead until this guy Snyder gets back from Europe, or until the smell in here is so bad it crawls out on the sidewalk.''

Beside me, Lola Wirtz made a sound deep in her throat.

Overmire lifted one corner of his lips. "Hunh-uh. I'm still throwing that one out, mister. Come to think about it, though, you seem to know a lot about this mystery man. Let's hear about him some more.''

I shrugged. "It all goes into my report to His Grace, Lieutenant—if I ever get the chance to make it.''

He sat there and thought about it, chair tilted back an inch or two on its back legs, one hand braced against the table edge. Connie Benbrook lighted another cigarette, looked impatiently at the two of us, started to say something and then thought better of it.

The legs on Overmire's chair came down against the linoleum with a small thud. "You know, Pine, I'm beginning to learn about you. I think you'd level with a client where you'd hold out on the Department. If we didn't have company and it wasn't so late, I'd drop in on the Bishop with you and listen in while you made your report.''

"Sure. And if he didn't want you to, you'd show him your buzzer.''

"You know better than that. I wouldn't want to and I wouldn't have to. A man in his position doesn't go in for playing things cute.''

I brushed ashes off my tie and nodded at him. "It's not for me to say. He's in his office, or the bedroom next to it, waiting for his phone to ring. You want me to call him?''

"What's the number?''

"Wabash 9900. He'll answer.''

He stood up abruptly and went off down the hall. Lola Wirtz said, "Is he really going to hold us, Paul? For questioning, I mean?''

188        *John Evans*

"He's going to try to. He'll make it stick, too, unless the Bishop talks him out of it."

"The man's a fool!" Connie Benbrook said sharply. "If he thinks for a minute he can keep me——"

I said, "Play that record to him, Mrs. Benbrook, and you'll sweat off a few pounds before you're sprung."

Overmire was back minutes later. "He'd like to see us, Pine." He stressed the "us" slightly. He looked at Constance Benbrook and Lola Wirtz and frowned thoughtfully.

I said, "This won't take long. Let them come with us, Lieutenant. I don't think His Grace will mind."

Rain was still with us, dripping dully against the sills of the study windows beyond the lowered metal blinds. A tired water-soaked breeze crawled in under the one window that was open a crack and swayed the blind there, with a tiny clicking sound.

Light from the desk lamp furnished the room's only illumination. Light, mellow and soft, giving a sheen to the rich redwood paneling and gleaming on the glass of the bookshelves. In the shadowy corners loomed the huge globe on its redwood stand and the severe lines of the cabinet radio.

The strain of the past few days had left its mark on Bishop McManus. He was still courtly and dignified in the Old World way most clergymen are, but his mild blue eyes were weary and a little dull and the puffiness about them even more evident. He was fully dressed, wearing a fresh dickey and a spotless collar. A lock of iron-gray hair had slipped its moorings slightly and come down a quarter-inch on his forehead.

Lieutenant Overmire and I were sitting in redwood and tan leather chairs directly across the desk from him, with the women apart and further back. Introductions were over with and there was that moment of unwieldy silence you get when waiting for someone to trot out the first word.

The Bishop cleared his throat almost harshly, gave us a reserved smile by way of apology, and said, "You seem quite solemn, Mr. Pine. Just how bad is this going to be?"

That surprised me enough to glance around at Overmire. The lieutenant shook his head. "I merely asked His Excellency if he'd see us at this time of night, that the details would have to come from you."

I said, "Raymond Wirtz is dead and the manuscript gone, with no chance of getting it back. I'm afraid I threw this one into the stands for you, Your Grace."

He closed his eyes and the muscles of his throat moved. Nothing more. Then he was looking at me steadily and his voice was almost gentle. "Please don't distress yourself, Mr. Pine. I'm sure you did your best."

"I'd like to agree with you, sir. But I was three steps behind from the start, in spite of getting more help than I had any right to expect."

Silence. I was the center of attraction, the main event, the roasted apple in the pig's mouth. I lighted a cigarette and dropped the match in the exact center of the huge ashtray on the desk. I leaned back and blew smoke through my nose and brooded at myself.

I said, "Three people I know of, besides you, Your Grace, wanted that manuscript. Myles Benbrook was one—a very wealthy man but not so wealthy he'd pass up this kind of jackpot. He killed two men trying for it—Vito Postori and Sergeant Frank Tinney—then got the bony finger himself. Lieutenant Overmire has been told my idea of how and why Postori and Tinney died, and I'll pass over that now, if you don't mind."

"As you wish."

"Number two of the three is worth some time telling about," I said. "It was through him I learned about the third person. Number two has been on our side all along. He was out to get the manuscript and hand it over to you. A twenty-five-million-dollar gift."

He was staring at me like a lady missionary at her first

heathen. "Mr. Pine, I haven't the slightest idea what you're talking about."

"There's no way you could. His name, Bishop McManus, is Louis Antuni."

Both Overmire and the Bishop gaped at me and mumbled their surprise.

I waited until they recovered, then said, "Antuni's an old man and a dying man. He's got a hospital full of things wrong with him and very little hope of a glorious resurrection."

Overmire said, "I'll be god——" He caught himself, coughed and started over. "This thing is really a dilly. I never thought I'd see the day when Mr. Big showed up in this town again. What is this manuscript, anyway?"

I said, "Something holy is the best way to describe it, I guess. Which is why Antuni wants it. He wants to buy himself a halo and a harp, just as he used to buy State's Attorneys, judges and jurors. He thinks the kind of life he's led won't lead to salvation unless the Church intercedes for him. So he figures if he can do something big as penance, the Church will go to bat for him."

"That is a fallacy, Mr. Pine," the Bishop said soberly. "A man's salvation rests between him and his Maker. Sincere atonement is all that matters."

"Sure. But when it comes to such things Antuni is a simple soul. He wants insurance—and to him a Solemn Requiem High Mass is that insurance."

He sat there, marveling over the story. "Incredible," he murmured. "Louis Antuni, whose black deeds have become legends. I think I should like to meet him, Mr. Pine. The man needs spiritual guidance, if for no other reason than peace of mind."

"Guidance," I said, "would be fine. But nothing's going to satisfy him except that manuscript."

More silence. The Bishop cleared his throat harshly, leaned back to open the center drawer of his desk and took out a throat lozenge wrapped in silver paper.

While he was peeling it, Overmire crossed his legs the other way and said, "We've gotten off the track, I think. Who's this third party Louie told you about?"

I put cigarette ashes in the tray and leaned back again. Off to one side of where I was sitting, Lola Wirtz and Connie Benbrook were quiet and beautiful in their chairs. As nice as the Bishop's study was, the two of them added something worth while to the place.

"From here on in," I said, "I'm going to sound like Eric Ambler with a hang-over. It couldn't miss sounding that way when you consider a twenty-five-million-dollar prize is pulp fiction all by itself.

"Louie gave me the name of a party to watch out for. A storybook crook, whom no one can describe or tell anything about. You'll have to remember Antuni knows a lot of people all over the world—most of them crooks themselves, I suppose—who think a lot of Louie and keep him posted."

I yawned before I realized one was coming up. For some reason that yawn right then made the whole idea of an international crook seem a little ridiculous. The Bishop peeled himself another lozenge from the middle drawer and Lieutenant Overmire rubbed the side of his neck, rasping the stiff hairs there.

"Antuni," I said, "called this modern Raffles—to coin a phrase—Jafar Baijan. He even went so far as to say it could be a man *or* a woman; that's how undercover Baijan really is. At the time I laughed at him—to myself—for saying it.

"Anyway, Antuni told me Baijan has been on the trail of this manuscript for quite a while. He traced it to Los Angeles, where it passed into Wirtz's hands, followed Wirtz to this town and found him at once. Don't ask me how; I'm told he's smarter than you or I or Einstein.

"He tailed Wirtz here to the rectory and he tailed him to Benbrook's. What scared him the most, I would say, was having Wirtz come here. That told him where the guy expected to sell the manuscript, and he knew if you ever got your hands on it, he was out of luck entirely. The manuscript would end up in the Vatican's vaults and not even Jafar Baijan could pry it out.

"But you were out of town, Your Grace, and that gave Baijan a two-week breathing spell. He must have made some effort during that time to learn where Wirtz had stashed the manuscript; it was too big to carry in a pocket and for that reason must have been hidden somewhere. Just where we'll never know."

I got up and walked up and down to keep my legs from going to sleep. Lola Wirtz gave me an uneven smile but avoided my eyes. I figured I knew why. The two men watched me, frowning a little, wanting to ask questions but not knowing just what questions to ask.

I sat down again and lighted another cigarette, just for something to do, and went on flapping my jaw.

"Then," I said, "the same day Wirtz made his second call at the rectory and talked to you, Your Grace, Jafar Baijan lost him. Then I came into the case and got my name in the paper and that would make it a cinch he knew about me—if he hadn't before then. He found out about Wirtz's car being in the Cushman Garage about the same time I did, I'd say.

"The night I followed Wirtz's car, Baijan held onto my coattails. After the smash-up, he parked a block away and came up behind the wrecked Chevvy and listened in on my talk with Benbrook. He knew right away, naturally, that I was wrong in fingering Benbrook as Wirtz; and when it looked as though I was going to run the man in, he stepped out and sapped me.

"His idea might have been to force Benbrook into leading him to Wirtz—your guess is as good as mine. But Benbrook, nervous as a wet cat, grabbed my gun as I blacked out, and got himself shot for his pains."

They sat there, looking thoughtful and interested. Constance Benbrook was snuffling a little into a handkerchief from her bag, but her heart wasn't really in it. Overmire fumbled around in his pockets and came up with a bulldog pipe and a stained chamois tobacco pouch. He dug the pipe bowl into the pouch, tamped the flakes down with a stubby thumb and struck a kitchen match against his shoe sole. He puffed a time or two, blew out the match and got rid of it. He said slowly, "While he was at it, why didn't he blast you?"

"Don't sound so disappointed," I said. "Maybe because he hoped I might lead him to Wirtz. There's a lot of angles to this business I don't know and probably never will. I came here to make a report, not solve any murders. But I couldn't help picking up an idea or two along the way and I'm giving them for what they're worth. If anything."

Overmire glanced sideways at me and lifted an eyebrow. "End of the line, or do you have some more?"

I said, "When I walked into that house out on Grace Street tonight, I saw a couple of things besides Wirtz's body—two things, one leading naturally into the other, that made me see this whole picture from a fresh angle. On the surface it looked as nuts as a pecan orchard. But the more I thought it over, the more beautifully simple it became."

The lieutenant blew out a mouthful of smoke with an impatient snort. "You sound like you're trying out for Inner Sanctum. Spit it out, will you?"

I said, "To begin with, none of us knew where Wirtz was hiding out. Benbrook was dead; he couldn't lead anybody there. Then I got my brainstorm, called Mrs. Benbrook to check on that address, then went tearing out there myself, with Lola Wirtz for company. Yet, according to Mrs. Benbrook, Wirtz was dead when she walked in a few minutes ahead of Mrs. Wirtz and me."

Constance Benbrook was out of her chair. "He *was* dead, you fool! Don't think for a minute you can put the blame on me. I had no reason——"

I folded my arms across my chest and leaned back. "When I blame you for anything you'll know it. Sit down and keep out of this."

It left her with her mouth open and no words.

While she was sinking back into her chair, I said, "If Jafar Baijan is the one who killed Wirtz—and you'll never convince me he wasn't—and since no one was still living who could lead him there, there's only one answer you can get: Wirtz must have telephoned Baijan and told him where he was hiding."

No one said anything but their expressions indicated they'd fallen off on that last curve.

"That," I said, "was number one of the things I realized. The second had to do with a mistake both Louie Antuni and I made, the mistake of assuming Jafar Baijan would see my name in the paper and get in touch with me. You see, Jafar Baijan had already contacted me— in fact, I was working for him."

Bishop McManus smiled gently. Still smiling he put his hand in the drawer among his lozenges and brought out a gun.

It was coming up fast when I unfolded my arms and shot him through the head.

# · 15 ·

It was beginning to get light over to the east across the lake. A long way from dawn yet, but still the hint of a dawn was there. Up on the fifth floor of Central Station, on the Wabash Avenue side, there were no buildings between me and the horizon, which was why I could see so far.

There were three of us sitting in Overmire's private office up there. Connie Benbrook had been sent home in near hysterics, leaving Lola Wirtz to see me through the tough hours ahead. Nobody was going to send her home—Overmire had tried it and so had I. But she stayed, and was still there when I was finished with dictating reports and going from room to room.

The lieutenant came out of a silence to say, "I still can't see how in hell he expected to get away with a crazy impersonation like that. A bishop, man! Bishops know a million and twelve people. Theirs is a highly specialized profession, if you can call it that. How did this guy expect to get away with it?"

My throat was hoarse from talking, but it seemed it was going to be a lot hoarser before I had a chance to rest it.

I said, "Look, the guy was really smart. You don't get to be a crook of that stature unless you've got more guts and imagination than any twelve people should have. In the first place, he expected the impersonation would last only one day. Why? Because he had followed Wirtz

to the rectory two weeks before the real bishop got back
from New York, or wherever he was. He knew Wirtz
would be back the first day the bishop returned. So he
went East himself, intercepted the real Bishop McManus,
studied his mannerisms, voice and appearance. It was a
break for him that they resembled each other in a loose
sort of way—as a lot of men around the same age and
general build do. Believe me, if they hadn't had that
same general appearance, Baijan would have found some
other method of pulling a coup. Then when the time
came for Bishop McManus' return, Baijan killed him
and got rid of the body."

"But to fool people who knew him intimately—even
for one day!"

"Think a minute," I said. "All bishops look alike,
in the same way all harness cops look alike. You see the
uniform, not the man behind it. Where was Baijan's
greatest danger of failure? His secretary and the woman
at the reception desk. Easy to do, Overmire. He called
up from the station the minute he arrived in town and
ordered his secretary to take his vacation immediately;
he went through the reception room fast, up to his office.
And there by God he stuck—except for the couple of
nights when he snuck out to kill Benbrook and Wirtz.

"Why, even when he got panicky enough to call in a
private investigator to find Wirtz, he couldn't be sure he
wasn't getting hold of some friend of the real Bishop's.
When he first called me he asked if we hadn't met and
I said no. But I wasn't in his office ten minutes the next
day before he brought up the question a second time,
just to be sure.

"Yet with all these precautions, he damned near threw
a shoe. That old maid receptionist has pretty close to a
camera eye. My first day on this case she told me Bishop
McManus was a changed man, that he was older and
thinner and had new lines in his face. She put it down
as due to his being worried about something—just as I

did when I heard his story about that manuscript. But that was stupid of me Lieutenant. The thing I forgot is that he came in off the train looking that way, according to his receptionist's own statement. How could he have been worrying about that manuscript *before he had any way of knowing about such a thing?* Why, hell, I myself noticed he'd worn his hair parted on the side up until recently. Shave a spot on top for approaching baldness, a bit of face wax here and there—and he's in. Look, it *can* be done—he did it.''

I got up and went out and down the hall to the washroom. I could hear a drunk yelling away off some place in the building. Men with a hard manner and suspicion in their eyes passed me in the hall. Not hard and suspicious because of me; they were always that way.

When I came back they were still sitting the way I had left them. Overmire was back with his pipe again, not getting much joy from his tobacco to judge from his expression.

I sat down and put my feet up on an empty chair. "I'd like to go home, Lieutenant Overmire. I really would.''

"Sure, sure.'' He rubbed the back of his neck with slow care. "I'd still like to know where he stashed that manuscript.''

"Maybe he didn't get it,'' I said.

His mouth fell open. "What kind of a crack is that? You, yourself, told me he wouldn't have killed Wirtz without getting it first.''

"I don't think Wirtz had it with him,'' I said. "I do think Wirtz called him at the rectory and asked that he come out and get it. I think he told Baijan where it was and convinced him he was telling him the truth. You see, Lieutenant, if Wirtz had handed Baijan that manuscript, I don't think he'd have ever gone back to the rectory. But my guess is that he meant to go out some time this morning, pick the thing up and then blow town.''

"Then why kill Wirtz at all?''

I grinned at him. "Are you going to let me do all the work?"

He glared at me and repeated the question.

"I'll have to guess," I said, "but I think I can make it sound reasonable. Baijan, forced to wait until morning to get actual possession of the manuscript, might have been afraid Wirtz would reconsider and block him off at the last minute. Or, once Baijan, as the Bishop, disappeared, Wirtz would have realized he'd been snookered and he might let out a yell. This way, with Wirtz dead, Bishop McManus' disappearance would have been a nineday wonder, period. Nobody would have known about Jafar Baijan."

I let my feet slip off the chair, then stood up and took my hat off his desk. "Time's up. If you think of any more questions, write 'em down. When I'm retired and busy with my memoirs, come around and ask me. Come on, blondie."

At the door, I turned around and looked back at him sitting there. "You know why it took us so long to see the answer, Lieutenant? Because we thought of Baijan as a bishop instead of a man. A man—any man—can be a killer and open to suspicion. But not a bishop; by the very nature of his calling he's above such flaws. All of us—no matter how calloused we get from rubbing against the wrong kind of people—never look on the clergy with the eyes we have for ordinary people. We give them a halo, which is as it should be. But this time we gave a halo to the wrong man. This time it was a halo for Satan.

"I have made a speech. Good morning, Lieutenant."

She came by for me at twelve o'clock, as arranged, and we walked down half a block from the Dinsmore Arms' entrance and got into the Plymouth. The rain had stopped about four but the sky was still the color of a grammar school blackboard.

While I was starting the motor, she said, "Where are we going, Paul?"

"Didn't I tell you while we were on the way home from Central Station a few hours ago?"

"You know you didn't! You just said to drop around about noon and we'd go for a ride."

"All right. There's your answer."

"I don't see why you have to be so secretive about it."

"Who's secretive?" I turned west into Pratt Boulevard. "I've got a kind of a job to do and I thought you'd like to go along and watch me play detective."

Air through the open car window moved the shining glory of her hair. She said soberly, "Something to do with Raymond's death, Paul?"

"His and five others, counting the two bishops. A lot of blood, Mrs. Wirtz."

"But it's all over with now. Isn't it?"

"The killings? I think so."

"Then——"

I said, "You came to this town for something, Mrs. Wirtz. And I don't mean to deliver a gross of compassion for the bewildered man you married."

"Paul!" Her fingers bit into my right arm and her eyes were glowing. "You mean the manuscript? You know where it is? Is that where we're going?"

I pulled up at a stop light set against us. "You're giving me a bad opinion of widows, you know that, don't you? When a husband dies, isn't his wife supposed to go around with swollen eyes and a black-edged handkerchief clutched in her trembling fingers?"

She took her hand from my arm and let it drop to her lap, turning her face away. "Don't joke, Paul. I do feel terribly depressed by Raymond's death. But I didn't love him and we were separated this last year. I've told you that."

"Yeah." We started moving again, past a small lake at the intersection, a reminder we'd been having rain and might have more of it any minute. "You're the only client I have left, Mrs. Wirtz, and I'm on the job. When Lieutenant Overmire dropped in at my apartment yesterday afternoon while you were there, he said something—something that makes me think I may be able to come up with this manuscript after all. If I do get it, you, as Raymond Wirtz's widow, have a claim against it. But I'm not going to turn the thing over to you."

Anger and panic struggled in her lovely face. "But you have to! It's mine! I've thought of nothing else. . . ."

"I know. Twenty-five million bucks can get in the way of most anything. But it isn't money so far, Mrs. Wirtz; it's just some pieces of paper. I'm going to turn the manuscript over to Louie Antuni and you'll get your money from him. Maybe not right away and certainly not that much. You can go back to Los Angeles and sit on your patio, and one day the mailman will drop around and make you rich. *If* I can find the thing to begin with."

She said tightly, "You don't have the right to make deals with something that belongs to me."

I said, "Let's not be technical. Actually that manuscript didn't belong to your husband to begin with. Would you like it to go into the police files and lie there while efforts are made to find the real owner?"

She was silent for several blocks. Then: "Why are you doing it this way, Paul?"

"I made a promise to Louie Antuni. I like to keep my promises, Mrs. Wirtz. Louie gets his Heavenly passport and I get my fifty thousand dollars. I'm a rich man, Mrs. Wirtz."

"I wish you'd stop calling me that!" She was smiling at me now, and her shoulder was pressing against mine. "You're also something pretty wonderful—and a little frightening. You . . . could have quite a honeymoon with fifty thousand dollars."

"Sure. But you need a woman for a honeymoon."

"I'm a woman, Paul." I barely heard her.

I smacked my lips. "Just think: poor, hard-working Pine, the people's punching bag, married to an heiress."

"I didn't say anything about marriage—just a honeymoon."

"I ever tell you about my school days?" I said. "Football was my dish; one of the best pass throwers in the league. But I always threw them, Mrs. Wirtz. I wasn't much good at catching them."

Silence the rest of the way.

I turned into a quiet street lined with look-alike houses and drew into the curb in front of one not far from the corner. Red brick, green trim at the windows and door, neat lawns where they belonged.

I went around and opened Lola Wirtz's door for her and we went up the walk and onto the porch.

A brown-haired woman, about thirty-five and willing to look it, opened the door to my ring. She was lovely enough to get herself stared at, dressed in a flowered print. She looked questioningly at Lola Wirtz and me standing there.

I said, "My name is Pine, Mrs. Taylor—if you are Mrs. Taylor?"

"I'm Irene Taylor, Mr. Pine. What was it you wanted?"

I had already seen what I hoped to see: a redness to her eyelids and indentations in her lower lip where her teeth had bitten.

I said, "I'm a private detective, Mrs. Taylor. This is Miss North, my secretary."

Irene Taylor's eyes became suddenly guarded. She started to say something, stopped, saw the expectant look on my face . . . and stepped aside.

"Please come in."

We went into a modest-sized living room, furnished sparingly with period pieces. There were the remains of a small fire behind the screen of a tiny fireplace, and two red bowls of sweetpeas on the white mantel.

When Lola Wirtz and I were sitting on the couch across

from her, I said, "I'd like to extend my sympathies, Mrs. Taylor."

She tried to act surprised, but her grief was too recent and too real to let her bring it off.

I nodded. "I mean Raymond Wirtz, of course. While I never met him personally, we had some mutual acquaintances."

Lola Wirtz was sitting as stiff as a Puritan's conscience, staring at the other woman and digging her fingers into the gray leather bag in her lap.

"How did you know?" Irene Taylor whispered. "But you couldn't! Not even Myles Benbrook knew."

I said, "I didn't know, really. Not until you opened the door to us. But you'd been crying, Mrs. Taylor—something the death of Myles Benbrook hadn't made you do. When Lieutenant Overmire told me that, yesterday, I wondered about it."

She looked at me stonily. "Myles Benbrook was never any more to me than a wonderful friend, Mr. Pine. I was his secretary for years, and when he closed his business he gave me this house as an expression of appreciation for those years."

"And Raymond Wirtz?" I said.

"I loved him, Mr. Pine—from the moment he walked in that door with Myles four days ago. I knew he was afraid of something or someone, but he never told me. He could have, because there wasn't anything I wouldn't have done for him."

Lola Wirtz said, "I wonder if you know, Mrs. Taylor, that——"

I had a hand on her shoulder by that time and her rush of words stopped sharply when my fingers bit in.

I said, "While Mr. Wirtz was here, he left something with you, I believe."

The guarded look flooded back into her eyes. "Left something with me? I don't believe I——"

I said, "Think a minute, Mrs. Taylor. There wasn't

anyone else he could trust—not even Myles Benbrook. The possibility of his leaving it with you didn't really register with me until the police lieutenant told me how you took the news of Benbrook's death. I figured you were strictly for Benbrook—that if this thing ever got into your hands you'd see that *he* got it.''

Nobody said anything for a long moment. Lola Wirtz seemed to be having trouble with her breathing.

Finally I said, ''He did give it to you to hold, Mrs. Taylor?''

''Yes, Mr. Pine.''

I let a breath flow out of me. ''Thank you. I'll have to ask you to let me have it. I'll see that it gets into the hands of the person it should go to.''

She started to say something, then stopped with her mouth open when Lola Wirtz opened her bag and took out a Colt .25 revolver and pointed it at me. She was standing by this time and now she backed away where she could keep Irene Taylor covered too.

She said, ''I'll take that manuscript, Mrs. Taylor.''

There was a real silence now—the kind called stunned. I said, ''Is it because you're just impatient or have I missed something?''

That earned me a sneer. Even the gun muzzle seemed to sneer. ''This time you missed something, Paul,'' she said. ''I'm not Lola Wirtz—I just borrowed her name for a while. I let you think me as no more than a grasping ex-wife, whose compassion for her husband was obviously false. You were so completely self-satisfied with that answer that you didn't take the trouble to investigate me beyond that.''

''I hope it teaches me a lesson,'' I said. ''Just for the hell of it, what name shall I use when I go around telling people how you outsmarted me?''

Sneer number two. ''My name would mean nothing to you. I've been after that manuscript ever since Kurt was murdered by Jafar Baijan in Los Angeles. I'm the girl who came to America with Kurt. Antuni told you about me; weren't you listening?''

I didn't say anything.

Irene Taylor said, "I'm afraid you've made a mistake, Miss North.''

The quiet, completely indifferent way she said it straightened the blonde up like a left hook. "What does that mean?'' she said harshly.

"I don't have the manuscript now.''

The gun jerked a little and I felt the muscles of my legs tense to spring. "Don't lie to me!''

"I'm not lying.'' If Irene Taylor was frightened by that gun, better eyes than mine would have to see it. "Would you recognize the manuscript, Miss North?''

The blonde, hard lines in her face, took a slow step toward the other woman. "I certainly would! And if you're trying——''

"Then if you'll look in the fireplace you'll find what little is left of it. When I learned Raymond Wirtz was dead, I made up my mind his murderer would never get what he was after. I burned that manuscript not more than twenty minutes before you came in.''

I thought Lola North was going to faint where she stood. Then she was across the room and sweeping the fire screen aside. She bent, keeping the gun barrel and one eye more or less on us, and poked at the small blaze there, mostly ashes now, with a brass poker.

When she straightened again, the poker clattered to the bricks and all color was gone from her face. "You fool!'' she cried. "Do you realize what you've done? Didn't you know what it was?''

Nothing changed in Irene Taylor's face and her voice was as indifferent as before. "Raymond told me it was something very old and very valuable. I didn't ask any questions and that was all he said about it.''

"Valuable?'' The blonde's voice cracked in the middle of the word. "It was worth millions, you—you——''

Irene Taylor seemed not to be listening. I was watching the younger one, waiting for the reaction to set in—a reaction that might mean bullets for Mrs. Taylor and me.

The blonde turned, scooped up her bag, went quickly along the hall and out the front door.

I slumped back on the couch, talking to myself. Irene Taylor sat across from me and listened, a blank look on her face. When I ran down, she said, "Are you going to let her get away, Mr. Pine?"

"I couldn't do anything else if I wanted to. She hasn't done anything to be nabbed for."

"But she tried to get the manuscript!"

"She didn't get it. All she did was worm her way into my confidence and they don't go to jail for that. . . . Uh—you really burned it, Mrs. Taylor? All of it?"

"Yes, Mr. Pine."

It was impossible not to believe her. "This," I said, "is the damnedest thing. And yet it couldn't hardly have turned out any other way. Well, good-by, Mrs. Taylor. You are a wonderful woman."

All the way back to the Loop my thoughts were on Louie Antuni and how he was going to take the news. Take all hope of Heaven away from a man like that, a man who all his life has had but one answer for people who let him down, and you know what to expect.

I saw myself walking into that small brick bungalow out on the West Side and facing him across the desk of that steam-heated room. I heard myself saying, "It was a great dream while it lasted, Louie. Only it's over now and there'll be no golden streets for you."

It could earn me a barrel of cement for my legs and the Drainage Canal for a tomb. At best it would cost me my fifty grand. It seemed a trifling amount.

At one-forty-five I was downtown and turning the Plymouth over to an attendant at the parking lot. He looked at my expression, grunted and drove the car up the ramp and away. I went on down Wabash to Jackson Boulevard and stopped at the corner newsstand for the latest edition of the *Daily News*.

For a long time I stood there staring at the headline while the man held out my change. He said, ''You want your money, mister?''

I shook my head and moved over to the curb. While waiting for the light to change, I looked at the headline again.

### FORMER GANG LORD DIES IN SLEEP

I folded the paper and stuck it under my arm. Off to the east the clouds were breaking up. No more rain for a while. I stood there looking at that patch of blue. Up there somewhere was the place Louis Antuni had tried to buy a ticket for.

Maybe they had let him in without one.

There is an extensive list of NO EXIT PRESS crime titles to choose from. All the books can be obtained from Oldcastle Books Ltd, 18 Coleswood Road, Harpenden, Herts AL5 1EQ by sending a cheque/P.O. (or quoting your credit card number and expiry date) for the appropriate amount + 10% as a contribution to Postage & Packing.

Alternatively, you can send for FREE details of the NO EXIT PRESS CRIME BOOK CLUB, which includes many special offers on NO EXIT PRESS titles and full information on forthcoming books. Please write clearly stating your full name and address.

## NO EXIT PRESS Vintage Crime

Classic crime novels by the contemporaries of Chandler & Hammett that typify the hard-boiled heyday of American crime fiction.

### FAST ONE — Paul Cain £3.95pb, £9.95hb

Possibly the toughest, tough-guy story ever written. Set in depression Los Angeles, it has a surreal quality that is positively hypnotic. It is the saga of gunman-gambler Gerry Kells and his dipsomaniacal lover, S Granquist (she has no first name), who rearrange the L.A. underworld and disappear in an explosive climax that matches their first appearance. The pace is incredible and the complex plot, with its twists and turns, defies summary.

### SEVEN SLAYERS — Paul Cain £3.99pb, £9.95hb (available 11/88)

A superb collection of seven stories about seven star crossed killers and the sole follow up to the very successful Fast One. Peopled by racketeers, con men, dope pushers, private detectives, cops, newspapermen and women of some virtue or none at all. Seven Slayers is as intense a 'noir' portrait of depression era America as those painted by Horace McCoy and James M Cain.

### THE DEAD DON'T CARE — Jonathan Latimer £3.95pb, £9.95hb

Meet Bill Crane, the hard-boiled P.I., and his two sidekicks, O'Malley and Doc Williams. The locale of the cyclonic action is a large Florida estate near Miami. A varied cast includes a former tragic actress turned dipso, a gigolo, a 'Babe' from Minsky's, a broken down welterweight and an exotic Mayan dancer. Kidnapping and murder give the final shake to the cocktail and provide an explosive and shocking climax.

### THE LADY IN THE MORGUE — Jonathan Latimer £3.99pb, £9.95hb

Crime was on the up. People sang of Ding-Dong Daddy, skirts were long and lives were short, violin cases mostly sported machine guns. Bill Crane thought it was a pretty wonderful time. He was in the Chicago morgue at the height of summer, trying to cool off and learn the identity of its most beautiful inmate. So-called Alice Ross had been found hanging, absolutely naked, in the room of a honky tonk hotel. His orders were to find out who she really was. Alice was stolen from her slab that night! Thus began the crazy hunt for a body and a name, through lousy hotels, dancehalls and penthouses, with occasional side trips to bed to bar to blonde and back again.

### MURDER IN THE MADHOUSE — Jonathan Latimer £3.99pb, £9.95hb

Hard drinking, hard living Bill Crane in his first case has himself committed incognito to a private sanitarium for the mentally insane to protect rich, little Ms Van Camp. Terror, violence and sudden death follow when a patient is found strangled with a bathrobe cord. The murderer strikes again but makes a fatal error in killing pleasant little mute, Mr Penny. The local police doubt Crane is a bonafide detective and believe he is suffering from delusions, the non-alcoholic kind. Despite all this, Crane breaks the case in a final scene of real dramatic fury.

### HEADED FOR A HEARSE — Jonathan Latimer £3.99pb, £9.95hb (available 9/88)

Death row, Chicago county jail. Robert Westland, convicted of his wife's murder, is six days from the 'chair'. What seems an iron clad case against Westland begins to fall apart as Bill Crane races against time to investigate the background of the major players and prove Westland's innocence. Westland's two brokerage partners; his hard drinking, hard riding cousin; enigmatic and exotic Ms Brentino; the amiable Ms Hogan; a secretive clerk; a tight-lipped valet and a dipso widow all have plenty to explain. Aided by a lime squeezer, a quart of whisky, a monkey wrench, a taxi cab, a stop watch and a deep sea diver, Crane cracks the case in this locked room classic.

**GREEN ICE — Raoul Whitfield £3.99pb, £9.95hb**
Watch out for Mal Ourney: where Mal goes, murder follows. It is on his heels as he walks out of Sing Sing after taking a man-slaughter rap for a dubious dame and follows him all the way on the trail of some sizzling hot emeralds — 'Green Ice'. "naked action pounded into tough compactness by staccato, hammer-like writing" Dashiell Hammett.

**DEATH IN A BOWL — Raoul Whitfield £3.99pb, £9.95hb**
Maestro Hans Reiner is on the podium, taking the fiddle players through a big crescendo. Then something goes off with a bang and it isn't the tympani! Reiner finds himself with a load of lead in the back — and a new tune: The Funeral March.

**THE VIRGIN KILLS — Raoul Whitfield £3.99pb, £9.95hb**
Millionaire gambler Eric Vennel's yacht sets sail for the regatta at Poughkeepsie with an oddball assortment of uneasy companions: Hardheaded sportswriter Al Conners; beautiful Hollywood ham, Carla Sard; Sard's nemesis tart-tongued scribbler Rita Veld; big ugly out of place bruiser Mick O'Rourke, and a glittering cross-section of east and west coast society. Rumours of Vennel's heavy betting on the regatta and a midnight attack by a masked intruder raise the tension . . . to the point of murder!

**HALO IN BLOOD — Howard Browne £3.99pb, £9.95hb**
Meet Paul Pine, Chicago P.I. Three seemingly unrelated events — the funeral of a pauper at which 12 clergymen from different faiths are the only mourners; Pine being hired by John Sandmark to dig up some dirt on the man intending to marry his daughter, Leona; and a run-in with the gangster, D'Allemand, where Pine is nearly killed delivering a $25,000 ransom in counterfeit bills — are woven into a complex and web of events that produces some explosive twists to the finale.

**HALO FOR SATAN — Howard Browne £3.99pb, £9.95hb. (available 9/88)**
Raymond Wirtz has something everyone wants! His grace, the Bishop of Chicago; Lola North, "a girl who could turn out to be as pure as an easter lily or steeped in sin and fail to surprise you either way"; Louis Antuni, Chicago Godfather; Constance Benbrook, who "wasn't the type to curl up with anything as inanimate as a novel" and mysterious super criminal, Jafar Baijan — all want what Wirtz has . . . the ultimate religious artefact. Private Eye, Paul Pine is right in the middle. In the middle of a deadly obstacle race strewn with corpses, cops and beautiful women.

**NO EXIT PRESS Contemporary Crime**

A companion to Vintage Crime in the popular pocket book forma
that highlights both the classic and exciting new books from the
past twenty years of American Crime Fiction. Contemporary Crin
will feature in 1989 such titles as Day of the Ram by William
Campbell Gault, Ask the Right Question by Michael Z Lewin,
Act of Fear by Michael Collins, Dead Ringer and Castles Burning
by Arthur Lyons all costing just £2.99.

**HARD TRADE — Arthur Lyons £2.99pb**
LA's most renowned detective, Jacob Asch is on the street once
more in a startling tale of Californian political corruption. A
troubled woman hires Asch to uncover the truth about the man
she is to marry. When Asch discovers the man is gay and the
woman is run down on her way to a hastily called meeting with
Asch, it becomes clear something big is at stake. Serious money
real estate schemes, the seamy side of LA gay life and a murder
frame involve Asch in a major political scandal that costs him his
licence and nearly his life.

**THE KILLING FLOOR — Arthur Lyons £2.99pb**
David Fein, owner of Supreme Packing, a slaughterhouse in a
grimy little Californian town had a problem . . . he was a com-
pulsive gambler. First he couldn't cover his losses from the takings
so he got a loan and went into debt. By the time he took in
Tortorello, a clean cut Harvard type but with 'Family' connections
he was in big trouble. Now he had been missing for 4 days and
his wife was frantic. Jake Bloom, old family friend puts her in
touch with Jacob Asch, who figures Fein is on a bender or in the
sack with another woman — he's heard and seen it all before.
But that's before he finds a body on the killing floor.